"Oh, grow up, will you, Dezzy!" Dee snapped. "You're thirteen years old, and you still act like a baby. And look at the way you dress."

"What's the matter with the way I dress?"

"You're such a slob. Either you run around in old sweats or you dress up in silly dresses that nobody else wears. All my friends laugh at you."

Dezzy's eyes filled with tears. "Who laughs at me?" she blubbered.

"And you cry over nothing." Dee lowered her voice. "Will you stop it? Everybody's looking at you."

Dezzy's nose began running, and she fished around in her sweatpants for a tissue. She didn't have one. Dee impatiently handed her one.

"Okay, okay, Dezzy, turn it off." She gave Dezzy a kindly pat on her arm. "I don't mean to hurt your feelings, Dezzy, but, honestly, you're not a baby anymore. You have to grow up."

"Told from Dezzy's point of view, the novel validates her uniqueness and her bravery in choosing to be different. . . . With her usual skillful characterization, Sachs ably captures the often painful disparity among young teens as puberty arrives unannounced."　　　　— *School Library Journal*

PUFFIN BOOKS BY MARILYN SACHS

At the Sound of the Beep
Circles
Class Pictures
Peter and Veronica
A Pocket Full of Seeds
Thirteen Going on Seven
The Truth About Mary Rose
Veronica Ganz
What My Sister Remembered

Marilyn Sachs

Thirteen

GOING ON

Seven

PUFFIN BOOKS

PUFFIN BOOKS
Published by the Penguin Group
Penguin Books USA Inc., 375 Hudson Street, New York, New York 10014, U.S.A.
Penguin Books Ltd, 27 Wrights Lane, London W8 5TZ, England
Penguin Books Australia Ltd, Ringwood, Victoria, Australia
Penguin Books Canada Ltd, 10 Alcorn Avenue, Toronto, Ontario, Canada M4V 3B2
Penguin Books (N.Z.) Ltd, 182-190 Wairau Road, Auckland 10, New Zealand

Penguin Books Ltd, Registered Offices: Harmondsworth, Middlesex, England

First published in the United States of America by Dutton Children's Books,
a division of Penguin Books USA Inc., 1993
Published in Puffin Books, 1995

3 5 7 9 10 8 6 4

The Library of Congress has cataloged the Dutton edition as follows:
Sachs, Marilyn.
Thirteen going on seven / by Marilyn Sachs. — 1st ed.
p. cm.
Summary: When her twin sister begins to assert her individuality and her
grandmother suddenly dies, thirteen-year-old Dezzy finds some comfort in
her relationships with her grandfather and a new friend and in an
interest in the environment.
 ISBN 0-525-45096-3
[1. Twins—Fiction. 2. Sisters—Fiction. 3. Individuality—Fiction.
4. Grandparents—Fiction.] I. Title.
PZ7.S1187Te 1993 [Fic]—dc20 92-44427 CIP AC

Puffin Books ISBN 0-14-037436-1

Printed in the United States of America

With love to the new kids—my grandnieces and grandnephews:

Chris, Adam, Deborah, Sari, Jesse, Andrea,

Jamey, Martina, and Clara

THIRTEEN GOING ON SEVEN

C H A P T E R

Dee didn't want a birthday party.

"Dezzy and I can each invite a friend to stay overnight," she told Mom and Dad. "I'll wear my Gap jeans and a ribbed T-shirt. We can have dinner at the Zuni Café, come home, listen to CDs, and sleep on the living-room floor."

"I want a party," Dezzy said. "I don't want to have dinner at the Zuni Café. I want to wear a new party dress, and I want to barbecue hot dogs and hamburgers like we always do—"

"Yuck!" Dee said.

"—on the deck, order a big cake with pink candles on it that says *Happy 13th Birthday, Dee and Dezzy,* and invite all our friends."

"You don't have any friends," Dee told her, "except for Rachel Castor Oil."

"Her name is Rachel Castori, and I have lots of friends."

"They all like me better," Dee said.

"No, they don't."

"Yes, they do."

"No!"

"Yes! And stop blubbering. It's disgusting how you cry over nothing. You're thirteen going on seven."

"Mom!"

Finally, they compromised. Mom said under no circumstances would she ever take four thirteen-year-olds to the Zuni Café. Maybe when they turned sixteen. How about each of them inviting a friend, going out to dinner at Bill's Hamburger—

"Yuck!" Dee said.

"—or to Vince's Pizzeria—"

"Yuck."

"—Or how about staying home and barbecuing chicken as well as hot dogs and hamburgers?"

4

"Okay, okay, we'll go out to Vince's," Dee grumbled. "I can always order something else besides pizza."

"And then we can come home, have a cake with candles, and sing 'Happy Birthday.' And you and your friends can listen to CDs and sleep on the living-room floor."

"I don't like to listen to CDs," Dezzy said, "but maybe we can all play Crazy Eights."

"Not me!" Dee said. "I stopped playing Crazy Eights when I was eleven. Besides, it's no fun playing with Dezzy. She always loses, and then she cries."

"No, I don't."

"Okay, okay," Dad said. "Whoever wants to listen to CDs can listen to CDs. Whoever wants to play Crazy Eights can play Crazy Eights. It's a free country. Everybody can do whatever he or she wants to do."

"And then we can have blueberry pancakes for breakfast." Dezzy's eyes were shining. "With Canadian bacon."

"Sounds good to me," Dad agreed.

"I'd rather have ricotta cheese and orange crepes," Dee said.

"And who's going to make them?" Mom demanded.

"We'll invite Grandma for breakfast," Dee suggested, "and she can make them."

"Sounds good to me," Dad said.

"Well, okay," Dezzy agreed, "and then, after, we can all go jogging with Dad."

Dad remained silent.

"Sounds good to me," said Mom. "You'll all go out jogging with Dad for a couple of hours, and I'll stay home and . . . and clean up."

"You mean you'll read the paper and take it easy." Dad shook his head. "No. I think you'd better come out jogging with us, too."

"Uh-uh," said Mom. "It's a free country, and I'd rather stay home and clean the house. Maybe Grandma will go jogging with you."

The party was a compromise. Dee invited Sara Hamada and Dezzy invited Rachel Castori. Dee wore her Gap jeans and her ribbed T-shirt, and Dezzy wore a new pink-and-white party dress. They ended up going to Chang's for Chinese food. Then they came home for the cake, listened to CDs and played Crazy

Eights, fell asleep after 2:00 A.M., and ate sausages and waffles for breakfast around eleven. After that, all the girls went out jogging with Grandma while Dad and Mom stayed home. Everybody had a good time.

Dezzy and Dee were twins. Their real names
were Desirée and Deirdre because a long, long time
ago, according to Grandma, back in Ireland, on
Grandpa's side, there had been another set of twins
called Desirée and Deirdre. Both had been beautiful,
charming, and . . . There was some disagreement
about what had finally happened to them. Grandma
thought that both married rich men, had many beautiful children, and lived happily ever after.

Grandpa said he didn't know what happened to
them, but Great-uncle Harvey claimed that Desirée

ran off with a traveling salesman and was never heard of again, while Deirdre married the local saloon keeper and danced barefoot on the bar.

Dezzy was older than Dee by three and a half minutes. She also weighed more at birth—four pounds, twelve ounces, to Dee's four pounds, three ounces. Both girls were kept in the nursery for a week, and then Dezzy came home. Dee had some breathing problems and stayed for another week. She turned out to be allergic to many foods. She also broke out in rashes and screamed most of the time for six months.

"But tell me about me," Dezzy always pleaded.

"You," Mom said, "you were a doll."

"More, more," Dezzy begged.

"You ate everything, and you slept through the night by the time you were a month old. And you smiled at four weeks and crawled early and walked before you were a year old."

"More! More!"

"And you spoke at a year. You said, 'Look at me!'—a whole sentence. And Dad and I couldn't believe it. You were so smart."

Dezzy loved to hear about herself from birth to six years old because at six Dee stopped being allergic and stopped breaking out in rashes. Before six Dee wheezed at night, and Dezzy remembered sleeping either with the sound of Dee's wheezing or the sound of the vaporizer humming. Dee, on the other hand, enjoyed hearing how everything changed at six. She didn't want to hear about what she was like before.

"Go on! Tell me!"

"Well, you always had spots on your cheeks and behind your knees and inside your arms. You used to scratch and scratch—"

"No, no!" Dee waved a smooth, strong arm without rashes. "No, no! Tell about how I grew and ate everything and caught up with Dezzy."

"Yes. Your appetite changed, and you could eat everything. You began to grow and grow." Mom laughed. "It was wonderful. Suddenly you grew taller than Dezzy, and you could run as fast."

"Faster," Dee corrected.

"And climb as high."

"Higher."

"And you filled out, and you just began talking and laughing. And you could read"—Mom clapped her hands—"you could read almost as soon as first

grade started. Not just *The Cat in the Hat* but everything. It was really amazing."

Dezzy tried to look happy whenever Mom or Dad
remembered how Dee changed when she was six. But
the memories didn't really make her happy. Because
Dee wasn't the only one who changed at six. She did,
too. If Dee grew taller than Dezzy, didn't that also
mean that Dezzy grew shorter than Dee? And if Dee
ran faster and climbed higher, didn't that also mean
that Dezzy ran slower and climbed lower? Mom and
Dad never said it that way, although Dee did. And
if Dee read so easily in the first grade, how was Dezzy
supposed to feel when she had struggled, and still
did, to bring meaning to those tormenting black
marks on the page.

Mom had gone back to school when Dee and Dezzy
were in first grade. She had taken courses to learn
how to become a reading specialist because of Dezzy.

"There is nothing wrong with your intelligence,"
Mom kept telling her. "Lots of people, brilliant peo-
ple, have learning disabilities and overcome them.
Einstein didn't even talk until he was five."

Sometimes Dezzy watched Dee when she was reading a book. She watched her eyes moving back and forth, back and forth across the page. She watched Mom when she was reading, and Dad when he was reading. Their eyes galloped nonstop over anything —newspapers, letters, books. She knew how she read, slowly, bumpily, fearfully, worrying if the next word would turn out to be a scary, unfamiliar one. The headaches began when she turned six.

"You've made wonderful progress," Mom said, "and I am really proud of you."

"I am, too," Dad said.

"Tell me about me when I was a baby," Dezzy kept asking.

Dee was tall, blond, blue-eyed, and looked like Dad. Dezzy was short, dark-haired, dark-eyed, and looked like Mom. At least most people said so. Dezzy hoped it was true, because Mom was pretty. Dezzy didn't think of herself as pretty. Mom's dark eyes sparkled. Hers just sat there in her head. Mom laughed a lot, and her forehead was smooth. Dezzy didn't laugh a lot, and she had lines in her forehead from trying to understand, especially from trying to understand those black marks on the white page.

"Relax," Mom kept on telling her. "You've made wonderful progress, and, remember, it has nothing to do with your intelligence. Einstein . . ."

Dee and Dezzy were always put in separate classes. Now, in the seventh grade, Dee had Ms. Ellison for her teacher, and Dezzy had Mr. Wong. Ms. Ellison and Mr. Wong decided to put on a joint Christmas/Chanukah pageant. Ms. Ellison picked Dee to play the part of a rock singer who has to sing "Jingle Bells" and gets all mixed up. Mr. Wong picked Dezzy to narrate the story of Chanukah while different people in the class sang Jewish songs and danced folk dances. Both girls were excited, maybe too excited. During rehearsals, whenever it was Dee's turn, Dezzy laughed so loud, you could hear her all over the auditorium.

Dee was very funny as she staggered around banging her head and singing:

> *Jingle bells, jingle bells*
> *Twinkle all the way.*
> *How I wonder what you are*
> *In a one-horse open sleigh-ay.*

"Calm down!" Mr. Wong told Dezzy. "You're making too much noise."

And whenever Dezzy got up on the stage and started telling the story of Chanukah, Dee made such funny faces that Dezzy never got further than "Chanukah, the festival of lights, celebrates . . ." before cracking up.

"Okay! That's it!" Ms. Ellison finally said. "Both of you, out of here! You're finished. You can sit outside the principal's office from now on during rehearsals."

Dee blamed Mr. Wong and Dezzy blamed Ms. Ellison. "You were the best one," Dezzy said. "Nobody was as funny as you." Dee didn't say Dezzy was the best, but she shrugged her shoulders and said she didn't want to be in the pageant anyway. "Me neither," Dezzy said.

The next day, Dezzy came down with the flu. She was out of school for a week. Grandma came over to stay with her and make soup and cookies. Mostly Dezzy just lay around watching TV and throwing up. Dee was especially nice to her. She even played Crazy Eights with her and lost.

When Dezzy came back to school, she discovered that somebody else was reading her part in the

Christmas/Chanukah pageant. It was Jordan King, and he mumbled and swallowed his words. Mr. Wong had shortened the narration and added more songs and dances. He said Dezzy could sit in the auditorium if she could control herself.

She would have if Dee hadn't been in the pageant—just as funny as ever, maybe even funnier.

"It's not fair," she told Mr. Wong. "If Dee is back in the play, then I should be, too."

"I didn't put her back in the play," Mr. Wong said. "And besides, you were sick for a whole week. We're giving the pageant next week, so I would have had to pick somebody else anyway. If you want, you can be one of the singers or dancers."

Dezzy didn't want to be one of the singers or dancers. "It's not fair," she told Dee. "You should have said no unless they took me back, too."

Dee shrugged her shoulders. "It wasn't my idea," she said, "but Ms. Ellison said I was so funny, everybody wanted me to do it. Nobody was as funny as me. And she thought since you were sick, you wouldn't be making any trouble."

"You made as much trouble as I did. You kept making faces. You—"

"Chill out, Dezzy!" said Dee.

Dezzy went home and cried. She cried all afternoon, and when Mom and Dad came home from work, she cried some more. "It's not fair," she told them. "Both of us were thrown out of the play. Both of us made trouble. Why should she get back in the play and not me?"

"Yes," Dad agreed. "It's not fair, and I think Dee should give up her part unless Dezzy is in the pageant, too."

"I won't," shrieked Dee. "I won't. I'm the most important person in the pageant. I'm the star. Everybody says so. I won't give it up. I won't. She's just jealous because nobody needs her."

"They do so need me," Dezzy yelled. "I'm very important. I tell the story of Chanukah. Mr. Wong put Jordan King in, and nobody can hear him."

"I'll talk to your teachers," Mom said.

Mom talked to Mr. Wong and Ms. Ellison, and Dezzy got her old part back. But then Jordan King's mother came to school, so Mr. Wong decided that both Dezzy and Jordan could share the part. First Dezzy narrated a few lines about Chanukah, and somebody sang a song and danced a dance. Then Jordan narrated a few lines, followed by another song and dance. Then Dezzy had another turn, and so did Jordan.

Dad showed up for the performance. Dezzy saw him sitting in the audience, and she watched his face when Dee came on. Dee wore a tight, shiny red dress, very short, sprayed with sparkles. She wore gobs of makeup and a funny purple wig. She shook and strutted all over the stage, roaring out her song. Dad doubled over laughing. Dezzy saw him and almost everybody else in the audience laughing and laughing and laughing. When she finished, the applause kept going on and on. Dee had to come out for an encore.

When it was Dezzy's turn, she could see Dad smiling and nodding at her. But other people in the audience were twisting restlessly in their seats, looking inside purses, or whispering to people next to them. Jordan messed up some of his lines, and she had to prompt him.

Afterward, Dee said she was great, but Dezzy didn't say anything to Dee.

3

Dee didn't really enjoy jogging. Sometimes she came along with Dezzy and Dad just to show that her stamina was as good as Dezzy's. Usually she preferred doing something else.

Dad was a serious jogger. He liked to go out very early in the morning, before anybody else was awake. Dezzy never could get up as early as Dad, but she could wait for him after work and go with him then. From the end of April until the middle of February, Dad came home from work no later than four. But between February and the end of April, the tax season, his hours were uncertain. Sometimes he didn't get around to jogging in the afternoons at all, which always made him restless and cranky.

Dad was an accountant. He was a partner in a firm called Rosenberg and Ryan. He was Ryan.

This afternoon, a cloudy, cool afternoon in early January, Dezzy waited for Dad in the kitchen. She was eating handfuls of cheddar cheese Goldfish crackers and trying to lace up her running shoes at the same time. She was the only one home. Dee and a couple of her friends had gone to the library. Dezzy was thinking about something she had heard at school today, and she was eager to talk to Dad about it. She gobbled up a final handful of Goldfish crackers and then focused on her shoes.

She heard the front door jiggle, which meant that Dad was putting his key into the lock. Dezzy leaped up and hurried to open the door, even before Dad had finished turning the key. "Oh, Dezzy," Dad said, looking surprised. "Are you waiting for me?" Dad always asked if she was waiting for him, although most days of the week he knew she was. Dezzy didn't want to think that Dad might prefer to go jogging by himself. After all, he did go alone in the mornings.

"Uh-huh," she said, "and Mom left a note saying we should pick up something for dinner. She's going to a meeting, and she won't be home until six."

"I'll change my clothes," Dad said. "I won't be long."

The day was cold and damp. Dezzy shivered as they began jogging, but after they reached the park, she didn't even notice the weather. They ran along Kennedy Drive and turned off the path to Stow Lake. She wasn't even winded yet, although Dad asked, "How are you doing?"

"Just fine, Dad," she said, and for a while, they continued jogging silently and comfortably together. Finally Dezzy began. "Dad," she said, "Mr. Franklin, my science teacher, said something."

"What?" Dad asked. They were circling the lake now, and another couple of joggers coming from the other direction smiled and nodded as they passed.

"He said . . ." Dezzy was beginning to feel the first signs of breathlessness. She knew that she would be ready to sit down in front of the boat house after they had completed the nine-tenths of a mile around the lake. She would sit there and wait for Dad, who might circle the lake several more times before the two of them headed back home.

"He said . . . some people thought . . . you could train a person to be a genius."

"Hey, look, Dezzy!" Dad cried. "I think there's a snowy egret out there in the middle of the lake."

"He said there was a girl . . . she's only fifteen . . . who's a great chess player. He said her father . . ." Now Dezzy was beginning to slow down, and Dad slowed down, too, even though he was jogging a few feet in front of her.

"Concentrate on breathing, Dezzy," Dad said. "Don't talk now."

So Dezzy didn't finish telling Dad what she had started until after they came home, showered, dressed, and started out by car to go shopping.

"I wanted to tell you, Dad," Dezzy said inside the car, "about this fifteen-year-old girl who's some kind of chess whiz."

Dad turned on the windshield wipers. "We lucked out, Dezzy," he said. "It's really raining now."

"Dad, this fifteen-year-old girl—"

"Oh, right. I read about her. She's a grand master, I think they call it. Anyway"—Dad chuckled—"she's really set the chess world on its ear. Women aren't supposed to be great chess players, and all those macho males are furious. Good for her!"

Dad nodded approvingly at Dezzy. Since he had

two daughters, he always approved of women who accomplished something.

"She has two sisters, Dad, and both of them are great chess players, too."

"Incredible!" Dad said. "Must be a very gifted family."

"But, Dad, that's just it. Mr. Franklin said the father of the girls decided before they were even born that he could train them—he could train any child —and turn them into something great."

"I don't know," Dad said doubtfully. "I think those girls must have been special to start with."

"Their father didn't let them go to regular school. He had special teachers teach them chess for five to eight hours every day, and then they spent a few hours on schoolwork and some time on phys. ed., and Mr. Franklin said they also had to spend about a half an hour telling jokes so they wouldn't end up weird."

"A half an hour?" Dad asked. "A half an hour a day?"

"Uh-huh."

"But what would happen if they needed three-quarters of an hour? Say they were telling a long joke and needed a little more time?"

"I don't know, Dad, but I was wondering. Do you think . . . ? Suppose I . . ."

"I think," Dad said, driving into the parking lot, "that the whole thing is pretty weird. I think that father should be brought up on charges of child abuse. Imagine giving kids a half an hour a day to tell jokes. What kind of creepo could he be?"

They bought broccoli, mushrooms, and red peppers for stir-fry, and a pound of shrimp. They also bought some vanilla fudge ice cream for dessert. Dezzy didn't continue her conversation with Dad, because she could see he would never agree to her staying home from school and learning to be a chess whiz.

Sunday morning Dezzy woke up feeling terrible. She went to the bathroom and immediately burst into tears. Then she stood outside Mom and Dad's bedroom, sobbing—not quietly. Nobody stirred inside, but Dee came out of the girls' bedroom, rubbing her eyes.

"What is it?" she asked sleepily. "What's wrong?"

"I want Mom," Dezzy wept.

Dee took her firmly by the hand and yanked her back into their bedroom. "Shh! You'll wake them up. They didn't get to bed until late last night. Don't you remember? They were out at a fortieth birthday party for their friend Laura, and—"

"I don't care." Dezzy continued to weep. "I want Mom. I need Mom."

"What's wrong? What is it?"

"It's all over my pajama bottoms," Dezzy cried. "And I don't know what to do."

"Is that all?" Dee shook her head. "You're just getting your period. That's all. No big deal."

"I don't want to get my period," Dezzy sobbed. "I don't want it."

"Well, you don't have any choice in the matter." Dee began poking around in their closet.

"I hate it!" Dezzy cried. Her face was slimy with tears.

Dee pulled out a pink box. "Here it is. Let's go back into the bathroom, and I'll show you how to put it on."

Dezzy stopped crying. "How come you know? You don't have a period."

"Well, I listened to the nurse when she talked to us at school. You heard her, too. Didn't you listen?"

"I listened," Dezzy admitted, "but I didn't think it would happen to me—not for a while—not for a long while."

"It happens to all girls," Dee said. "It means you can have babies now."

Dezzy started crying again. Loud. "I don't want babies now," she shouted.

"You don't have to have babies," Dee yelled. "It just means you can, stupid. It means you're a woman. You don't act like one, but that's what it means."

Both of them were making so much noise that Mom woke up and came staggering into their room. "What is it? What's wrong?"

"Oh, Mom," Dezzy wept, "it's terrible. I hate it."

"She got her period," Dee yelled. "It's not fair. She's just a crybaby, and she gets her period ahead of me." Dee began crying, too. "I'm taller than she is, and I'm more mature, and she doesn't even want it."

"Doesn't want what?" Dad asked sleepily, following Mom into their room.

Dad went out jogging as soon as he could, and Mom spoke to them both in her calm teacher's voice. She explained the physiology of menstruation and urged them both to read the book on the subject she had bought for them some time ago. She made the whole business sound so boring that both Dee and Dezzy couldn't wait until she finished talking about it.

Dee said she wanted her own room.

"Why?" Dezzy demanded. "We've always shared a room. Why do you want one now?"

"I just do," Dee said. "It didn't matter so much when we were little, but now I need my own space."

"Impossible," Mom said. "There's only the little room Dad uses for his office. He needs that room."

"I know he does. I don't want that room anyway. I'll take the one downstairs in the basement."

"The guest room?"

"We hardly ever have guests." Dee waved her hand. "And if we do, I'll move in with Dezzy."

"But it's dark."

"I don't mind. And I can use the bathroom downstairs just for myself."

"But it's so far away from the rest of us."

Dee smiled. "That's what I like about it," she said.

Dezzy couldn't sleep. The first night after Dee had moved downstairs, Dezzy tossed around and around. Finally she got up and went downstairs to Dee's room. She opened the door and stood over Dee, asleep on the floor. She could still smell the new paint on the walls. Even though she couldn't see in the darkness, she made a face, remembering the colors. Each wall was painted a different color—white, orange, black, and yellow-green. Dezzy thought it looked ugly, and she hated the crazy rock posters Dee had hung up on the walls. Dee was sleeping on a mattress on the floor. There was no other furniture in the room, but Dee said she was saving up for a rug and some throw pillows. She said she had outgrown their bedroom furniture, and that Dezzy could have all of it.

Dezzy ran her tongue around her lips and remembered. She remembered how they always played together until they turned six. She remembered how their clothes matched. Mom and Dad decided that they would never wear identical clothes, but they often wore the same outfit in different colors. Dezzy usually wore red and Dee blue. They even had matching beach balls—Dezzy smiled when she remembered those beach balls. Grandma and Grandpa had bought them—hers was red with a blue Mickey Mouse and Dee's was blue with a red Mickey Mouse.

Dezzy remembered how they used to run after those balls, and how Dee used to cry, "Wait for me! Wait for me!" and how she always did. Most of the time anyway.

Dee kept right on sleeping, so after a while, Dezzy turned around and went back upstairs. I'm not going to cry, she kept telling herself as she walked upstairs, but she did anyway. Crying always made her feel better. The wet pillow underneath her face comforted her, and she finally fell asleep.

The family was getting ready to go to Grandma and Grandpa's house for dinner. Dezzy wanted to wear her yellow daisy dress with the floppy lace collar, her white tights, and her patent-leather pumps. She was standing in front of the mirror, twisting around inside the dress and wondering why it felt so uncomfortable.

Mom came into her room and looked at her in the mirror.

"I don't know, Dezzy," she said. "That dress . . ."

Dezzy twisted around some more. "Something's wrong with it," she said. "Maybe the zipper is stuck."

"No, darling." Mom smiled. She was wearing a bright red-and-pink flowered jumpsuit with a cerise T-shirt. "The dress is too tight on you."

"But I just wore it a couple of months ago to Rachel's birthday party."

"A lot can happen in a few months." Mom examined Dezzy's reflection in the mirror very carefully. "I think you need a bra, Dezzy. We'll go shopping next week."

"A bra?" Dezzy looked at herself in the mirror. She saw herself, but it wasn't exactly herself either. In the mirror, a girl was wearing a beautiful dress that scrunched over her chest in a funny way. The girl was frowning, wrinkling her forehead. That, Dezzy was used to. But there was something different about the girl, something Dezzy hadn't noticed before, or maybe she had but had not connected it to herself.

"Better take the dress off. Maybe the red striped one would fit. I think we'll have to stop shopping in the girls' department for you." Mom smiled at Dezzy's reflection and rested a hand on her shoulder. "My big girl," she murmured.

Dee and Dezzy both went shopping with Mom for bras.

"I don't like the way it feels," Dezzy said, wiggling around inside hers. It was a white one with a tiny pink rose in the center. "It's too tight, Mom."

"Here, I can loosen it," Mom said, moving the hook. "Does it feel better?"

"It feels funny."

"You'll get used to it, honey." Mom sighed. "We all do."

"But not everybody has to wear a bra. Lots of girls don't."

"That's true," Mom said. "But I think you're going to take after me. You're going to need a bra."

Dee was wearing an electric pea green bra. "How does this fit, Mom? Don't you think I should try an underwire one?"

Mom shook her head. "They don't make underwires in your size, Dee. Actually, you don't really have to wear a bra yet, if you'd rather wait."

"I do need to wear one." Dee's voice was shrill. "I do."

"Well, you can if you want to, but you're much smaller than Dezzy."

"I need one," Dee said angrily. "And I'm *not* smaller than Dezzy."

Sometimes now, Dezzy felt lonely. Before, when she and Dee shared a room, she hadn't felt lonely. Before, she might have felt sad or angry or confused, but not lonely.

"Dee doesn't sit with me in the lunchroom anymore. She and her friends sit away from me, and now, when they come over to the house, they go into her room and shut the door."

She and Dad were running through the rose garden one afternoon in early February. Dad hadn't come home until five-thirty, but she had been waiting for him.

"I'll talk to her," Dad said.

"No, Dad, don't talk to her. I don't want you to talk to her. Please, Dad."

"Okay, okay!" Dad said. "Look, Dezzy, those magnolias are beginning to bloom."

They turned left on the drive and ran toward the conservatory.

"Some of Dee's friends," Dezzy said, "used to be my

friends, too. But since Dee moved downstairs, they stopped being my friends."

"You have plenty of friends," Dad said. "Watch out for that biker! Doesn't he know this isn't a bike path? The jerk!"

"No, I don't, Dad. I don't have lots of friends. Just Rachel Castori—but she's always busy with her music lessons."

"Maybe you should take music lessons, Dezzy."

"Okay, Dad, maybe I should."

They ran along quietly for a while, and then Dezzy asked, "But what kind of lessons should I take?"

"Well, what kind of musical instrument are you interested in?"

Dezzy considered for a minute or so as they ran past the tree that had descended from one of George Washington's. "I'm not sure, Dad."

"Well, your mother used to study piano. That's a very useful instrument if you go into . . . well, if you go into teaching or . . . other fields."

"I don't know if I'm interested in piano."

"Well, what does Rachel study?"

"I think it's called a Spanish horn or maybe a French horn. It has a terrible sound. I don't think I want to study that." She began to feel breathless, and Dad told her to stop talking. Soon she had to sit down in front of the conservatory and wait for Dad, who planned on running around the tennis courts and the children's playground.

She watched some kids rolling down the big hill near the road, laughing and shouting to one another, and she felt very lonely.

By the middle of March, Dad had stopped jogging in the afternoons. Sometimes Dezzy waited for him until five or five-thirty before giving up. Sometimes he remembered to call and tell her he wouldn't be coming home until too late to go jogging. Downstairs, in Dee's room, she could hear the CDs and the girls laughing and screeching. Sometimes they came upstairs to get something to eat, and sometimes they carried the food downstairs. Sometimes one of the girls might ask Dezzy to come down, too. She always went when she was asked. Sometimes she'd just hang around the kitchen or the living room, waiting, hoping somebody would ask. They always sounded as if they were having a wonderful time, but all they ever did was listen to CDs, dance, and talk about boys.

"Why can't I go jogging by myself?" Dezzy asked Mom.

"Because the park isn't safe for one girl by herself."

"But there are always plenty of joggers out, and I'd stay on Kennedy Drive."

"No, Dezzy, absolutely not. You can go with a friend."

"I don't have any friends except for Rachel Castori, and she's always practicing."

"Well, Daddy will be finished with his clients' income tax returns in another month or so. Meanwhile why don't you . . ."

"What?"

"Hmm . . . Why don't you . . . I know what, Dezzy. Maybe you'd like to sign up for a course at the center."

"Okay, Mom, what?"

"Well, I don't know, Dezzy. How about . . . how about . . . volleyball?"

"I don't like volleyball."

"Okay then, you could take a painting course, or maybe dancing? How about dancing?"

"I wonder," Dezzy said. "I wonder if Grandma would come jogging with me?"

· · ·

Grandma liked to jog, but now that she had developed a bone spur in one of her ankles, she didn't go out as much as she used to.

"I used to jog all the time," she told Dezzy the next day, as the two of them headed out for the windmill in the park. Grandma was wearing her oatmeal-colored sweat suit with the blue-and-silver chevron on the jacket.

"I introduced Mickey"—Mickey, short for Michael, was Dezzy's dad's name—"to jogging. Your grandfather never showed any interest in physical fitness. It's a miracle that man is still alive. The only exercise he ever gets is flipping on the TV and flipping it off."

Grandma and Grandpa argued all the time. Actually, Grandma argued all the time with most people except for Dezzy, Dee, and Dad. Grandma argued with Aunt Mary, Dad's sister, and with Uncle Bill, Dad's brother. Grandma argued with Mom, and whenever they went out for dinner together, she argued with the waiter.

Grandma liked telling Dezzy about all the people who made mean, stupid, or rude remarks, and about how she straightened them all out. Today, while she was telling Dezzy about the dumb doctor who had examined the bone spur in her foot and wanted to charge her a fortune to operate, she began to pant.

"Grandma," Dezzy told her, "maybe you'd better sit down on this bench. I'll just run out to the windmill and come back for you."

Grandma was so breathless, she didn't even argue about the park not being safe for a girl jogging by herself. Dezzy ran until she reached the windmill, then turned around and headed back. From the distance, she could see Grandma sitting on the bench. Grandma looked small suddenly, and her hair was completely white. She looked different to Dezzy. These days, too many things looked different.

"Why are you crying?" Grandma clenched her fists and jumped up as Dezzy drew closer. "Did somebody do something to you?"

"No, no, Grandma," Dezzy sobbed. "I'm fine. It's just . . . I think I got something in my eye."

It's humiliating!" Dee looked around at the little children playing with a wooden Noah's ark. In one corner, a young mother was rocking a screaming baby in her arms.

"What's humiliating?" Dezzy asked. She was craning her neck to see the treasure chest that Dr. Kramer kept filled up for his patients. After the visit, each child could pick a gift for herself.

"It's humiliating that girls our age have to keep coming here to Dr. Kramer with all these . . . all these . . . babies. We're old enough to go to a regular doctor, not a pediatrician."

The treasure chest was inside, beyond the receptionist's desk, and it seemed filled up higher than usual. "I like Dr. Kramer," Dezzy murmured.

"Oh, Dezzy, what is the matter with you?"

"I like coming to Dr. Kramer." Dezzy reluctantly transferred her gaze from the treasure chest to Dee's face. "I like him better than Mom and Dad's doctor. He's so nice. He's like somebody in our family. He writes to us when we're away in camp, and he has our pictures hanging up and . . . and . . ." Dezzy grinned. "I still like to pick something from the treasure chest."

"Oh, grow up, will you, Dezzy!" Dee snapped. "You're thirteen years old, and you still act like a baby."

Dezzy transferred her gaze back to the treasure chest.

"And look at the way you dress."

"What's the matter with the way I dress?"

"You're such a slob. Either you run around in old sweats or you dress up in silly dresses that nobody else wears. All my friends laugh at you."

Dezzy's eyes filled with tears. "Who laughs at me?" she blubbered.

"And you cry over nothing." Dee lowered her voice. "Will you stop it? Everybody's looking at you."

Dezzy's nose began running, and she fished around in her sweatpants for a tissue. She didn't have one. Dee impatiently handed her one.

"Okay, okay, Dezzy, turn it off." She gave Dezzy a kindly pat on her arm. "I don't mean to hurt your feelings, Dezzy, but, honestly, you're not a baby anymore. You have to grow up."

Dr. Kramer examined Dee first and then Dezzy. He said she was fine, and that she should come back in a year for her next checkup. Dezzy could see Dee in the waiting room. Dee had her nose in a copy of *Seventeen* and didn't notice Dezzy standing by the treasure chest. Quickly Dezzy reached down and grabbed a Mickey Mouse balloon. She slipped it into her pocket before joining her sister.

Dee showed Mom a brochure.

"I want to go to this camp, Camp Cornell, this summer," she said. "It's a camp for the performing arts, and they spend the whole summer putting on productions. You learn to do everything. Sometimes you act, sometimes you handle the lights, do make-up, costumes. . . ."

Mom looked at the brochure. "It's down in southern California," she said.

"I know. We'd have to fly."

"And it's expensive. It's for six weeks, not just two weeks. That would really cost."

"But, Mom, just look at what I could learn about the theater." Dee tossed her hair. She was growing it long, and it came down to her shoulders now. "I want to be an actress. Lori Ferguson's cousin—she's an actress—teaches one of the courses at Camp Cornell. She says it's one of the best acting camps in the country. Please, Mom!"

"I don't know, Dee, we'll have to think about it. For the two of you, it would be a lot of money."

"I don't want to go," Dezzy said. "I want to go back to Camp Sierra. I love Camp Sierra."

"Oh, Dezzy!" Dee waved at her impatiently. "You'd love Camp Cornell."

"I love Camp Sierra," Dezzy repeated.

"Boring!" Dee snapped. "They do the same things every summer. You go on the same hikes, the same overnights, you swim in the same stream, you sing the same songs, eat the same food, meet the same people. . . ."

"I like that," Dezzy said. "I don't want to go to an acting camp. I want to go to Camp Sierra for two weeks and swim in the stream and jump off the big rock. Dee, you always have a good time when we go to Camp Sierra. Remember how we raided the boys' cabin last summer?" Dezzy began laughing. "And Maureen is coming back as a counselor. We both loved Maureen. Maybe we'll have her again."

"I am not going back to Camp Sierra," Dee said, "and if you want to go yourself, you go. I've outgrown it."

"But, Dee," Dezzy began, "it won't be any fun. . . ." She wanted to say, "It won't be any fun without you," but she didn't finish her sentence.

Dee turned back to Mom. "I want to go to Camp Cornell. I can go by myself. As a matter of fact, I'd like to go by myself."

Dad and Dezzy were jogging on a Sunday afternoon. Usually Dad just went out mornings on the weekend, but since the tax season began, and he had to give up most of his afternoon runs, he tried to jog twice on Saturdays and Sundays.

"Dee wants to be an actress," Dezzy said as they ran through the Rhododendron Dell. The flowers were open all the way—purple, red, pink, and white. Petals floated gently through the air. "She's growing her hair long."

"You have to do more than grow your hair long to become an actress," Dad said, "but I do think she has talent."

"I wish I had talent." Dezzy tried to hold back the tears that were threatening.

"Oh, you have talent, all right," Dad said.

"I don't think so." Dezzy struggled with the tears. "I never noticed any."

"You will one day." Dad gave her a quick smile. "There's no hurry. Much better to take your time, the way you're doing."

Dezzy began feeling better. She noticed a wonderful lilac-colored bush and said, "Oh, Dad, isn't that one pretty!"

"Sure is," Dad said. But he had something else to say, and he slowed down to run next to her instead of a few paces in front as usual. "Everybody has some kind of talent. Sometimes you just have to grow into it. Look at your mother. She didn't know she would be such a marvelous teacher until you and Dee were born. Just think about how great she is—how she keeps winning best-teacher awards—but she didn't realize she was so talented until—"

"Until I turned out to have a learning disability." Dezzy sighed. "I wish she could have found out about it without me being so stupid."

"Hey, Mickey," somebody yelled, "how're you doing?"

"Oh, hi, Ron. What's doing?"

"Let's keep moving," Ron urged. He was an older man, like Dad, running with a boy about Dezzy's age.

"This is my boy Joey. That your daughter?"

"Uh-huh. Dezzy—short for Desirée."

The four of them jogged out of the grove and along a path that passed a statue of Francis Scott Key.

"Joey needs to build himself up," Ron said. "He has weak ankles, and I keep telling him that jogging will improve his stamina."

"Oh, Dad!" Joey sounded crabby.

Dezzy looked at him sympathetically. It was terrible when parents talked about your weaknesses in front of other people.

"Nothing to be ashamed of, Joey. None of us is perfect."

"I'm tired." Joey stopped jogging and flopped down on the grass.

"Come on, Joey, let's just go as far as the lake. You can do it."

"You go!" Joey scowled. "I'm staying right here."

His father stopped and stood over him.

"Well, see you around, Ron," Dad called out over his shoulder as he and Dezzy jogged on together.

"What a jerk!" he said, after they had moved on out of hearing. "He really embarrassed that boy."

"He looks familiar," Dezzy said.

"Ron?"

"No, Joey. I think he goes to my school."

"Poor kid!" Dad said.

A few days later, when Dezzy was eating lunch by herself at school, Joey stopped at her table.

"You're Dezzy, aren't you?" he asked. "I met you in the park on Sunday."

"I remember," she said. Joey was carrying a tray with his lunch on it.

"Can I sit here?" he asked.

"Sure!"

Joey smiled, and Dezzy thought he looked a lot more cheerful than he had in the park.

"I hate my father," he said, and bit into his sandwich.

"You what?"

"I hate my father," he said, and opened a bag of potato chips. "Want some?" He held it out to her.

"I don't know anybody who hates his father." Dezzy took a few chips and looked at him curiously.

"You're lucky," he said. "Your father looks okay."

"Yes," Dezzy agreed. "He is okay."

"Well, mine doesn't let me live. He can't stand it that I don't like sports. He's ashamed of me. My brother—he's older—is on the track team, and my father used to be on the track team when he was in school. He thinks everybody in his family has to be on the track team."

"What about your mother?"

"They're divorced."

"I guess she didn't make the track team," Dezzy said.

Joey stopped chewing his sandwich and stared at her.

"Oh, I'm sorry," Dezzy said. "That was a stupid thing to say. I'm always saying stupid things. I'm sorry, Joey. I really am."

Joey swallowed the pieces of sandwich in his mouth. Then he smiled. "You know," he said, "that's pretty funny." He began laughing. "I think I'll tell my father that. You've got some sense of humor."

"I have?"

"She didn't make the track team." Joey kept on laughing. "That's a good one."

That afternoon, when Dezzy was lacing up her running shoes in the kitchen, hoping Dad would make it back in time to go jogging, Dee and her friend Megan Jackson came into the kitchen.

"Hi, Dezzy," Megan said in a very friendly voice.

"Hi, Megan."

Dee sat down next to Dezzy at the kitchen table. "How do you know Joe Carter?"

"Who?"

"Joe Carter. The boy you were talking to today down in the lunchroom."

"Oh, Joey!" Dezzy shrugged. "I met him in the park on Sunday."

"He's cute," Megan said.

"He is?"

"You mean you hadn't noticed?" Dee stood up. "You really are something, Dezzy."

But Megan invited her to join them downstairs in Dee's room, and she went. They played CDs and talked about boys. Dezzy kept hoping that Dad would get home in time to go jogging with her. But he didn't.

Everybody in the family worried about Grandpa. He ate all the wrong things. He had bacon and eggs and cinnamon toast dripping with butter every morning for breakfast, while Grandma ate granola and described how all the fat he consumed was choking up his arteries. He made himself two cheeseburgers every day for lunch or two grilled cheese sandwiches with Italian salami or two liverwurst and pickle sandwiches overflowing with mayonnaise. Grandma generally ate a fruit or vegetable salad with yogurt. For dinner Grandpa liked to grill a steak or pork chops out on the barbecue in the backyard, while Grandma ate a piece of lean fish or a slice of turkey with some more salad. She never cooked for Grandpa, because he hated the kind of meals she prepared.

Grandpa was overweight. His chest and belly met somewhere above his belt line and overflowed like the mayonnaise on his liverwurst sandwiches. He never walked. Most of the time he stayed home, now that he was retired, and watched sports on TV. Sometimes he met some of his friends in a bar and came home smelling of beer.

Grandma yelled at him all the time. She called him a couch potato, and she told him he should make sure to meet all his life insurance payments because she didn't want to be left a poor widow. Dad tried to point out to Grandpa that all the most respected health authorities recommended a low-fat diet for older people, and exercise. Aunt Mary sent him articles about cholesterol, and even Uncle Bill, who was overweight himself, tried to get Grandpa to eat a salad at least once in a while.

Grandpa hardly ever went to the doctor, but when he did go, the diagnosis was never good. He had high blood pressure, gout, stones in his gallbladder, and asthma.

So one night, so late it was actually morning, when the phone began ringing, a voice deep inside Dezzy's sleep said, "Grandpa! Grandpa! Grandpa!" The ringing went on and on. Finally the voice inside her sleep stopped. Dezzy woke up and jumped out of bed. The ringing had also stopped. Dezzy rushed into her parents' bedroom without knocking, panic spreading inside her.

Dad was listening to a voice from inside the phone. Tears were running down his face. Mom was reaching out to Dad and crying, "Oh, Mickey, Mickey, I'm so sorry!"

"Is it Grandpa?" Dezzy sobbed, leaping up onto the bed. "Did something happen to Grandpa?"

But it wasn't Grandpa. It was Grandma.

When Dezzy saw Grandma lying there in her coffin so quiet and calm with a kind smile on her face, she really understood that Grandma was dead. Grandma was the first dead person Dezzy had ever seen, and it wasn't what she had expected. She had been crying on and off ever since the phone call, but now, seeing

Grandma lying there dead, really dead, she began crying so hard, she could hardly see anything through her eyes.

"Stop it, Dezzy!" Dee whispered. "Stop carrying on like that. Think of Grandpa."

Grandpa was sitting in the funeral chapel all dressed up in a suit and a tie. He wasn't crying. He wasn't saying anything. People came up and whispered things to him, and he nodded but didn't speak.

Dee went up to Grandpa, bent down, kissed him, and said, "We'll miss Grandma so much, Grandpa. Nothing will be the same without her."

Grandpa just nodded and patted Dee's hand.

Dezzy tried to control herself. She tried to think of Grandpa, so she also bent down, kissed his cheek, and burst into tears.

Grandpa patted her hand.

"Oh, Grandpa," Dezzy sobbed as Mom and Dad moved in on her, "she won't have to worry about that bone spur anymore."

Grandpa shook his head and wrinkled up his face.

"Come over here, Dezzy," Mom murmured, taking her arm.

"The bone spur in her foot, Grandpa. She won't have to pay that dumb doctor to have it removed."

Mom's fingers tightened on her arm as Grandpa smiled. "Yes," he said, "she certainly won't have to worry about that."

Nothing changed after the funeral. Grandpa went back to sitting in front of the TV, watching sports programs, and cooking his own unhealthy meals. Dad stayed home and cried for a couple of days, but it was right in the middle of the tax season, so he had to pull himself together and go back to work. Aunt Mary and Uncle Bill tried to get Grandpa to go back home with one of them. Aunt Mary lived in Los Angeles and Uncle Bill in Dillon, Montana. Grandpa said no. Grandpa said everybody should go home and leave him alone. He didn't want anybody standing around and making him nervous. Mom asked him to come over and have dinner with them for a while. She even offered to cook him the things he liked. Grandpa said no. He said he just wanted to stay home and be left alone.

• • •

"Maybe Dezzy and I can stop over on our way home from school," Dee said to Mom one Monday morning, a couple of weeks after Grandma had died. "We can just see if he wants us to do anything like shopping or maybe a laundry."

"That's very considerate of you, darling," Mom said. "I'm sure he'd love seeing the two of you. Ask him if he'd like to come back for dinner, and if he says yes, you can pick up some steak and some frozen french fries."

They could hear the TV going when they rang Grandpa's doorbell. It took him some time to open the door, and Dezzy noticed that he began blinking as soon as the daylight hit his eyes. Inside, the curtains and shades were drawn all over the house. It was dark except for the light from the TV. When Grandma was alive, she never let him keep the curtains drawn.

"How-you-doing, Grandpa?" Dee asked cheerily.

"Fine, fine," Grandpa said, hurrying back to his TV.

The twins followed after him and sat down next to him on the couch. Grandpa was watching a base-ball game, and somebody must have hit a home run, because Grandpa chuckled and said, "Pow!"

"Grandpa," Dee said, "Mom wants you to come for dinner tonight. We'll have steak and french fries," she added quickly.

Grandpa shook his head, but kept his eyes on the set. "No," he said. Then, after a moment, "Thanks." Then, after another moment, "Tell her thanks."

The girls sat quietly for a few more minutes. Then Dezzy asked, "Grandpa, can we look at the old photos?"

"What old photos?" A commercial break came on, and Grandpa turned to look at them, a puzzled expression on his face.

"The photos Grandma keeps . . . kept . . . upstairs in your bedroom closet."

"Oh!" Grandpa said. He turned back to watch the commercial.

"Can we, Grandpa?"

"Oh, okay. You know where they are?"

"Sure." She stood up, and Dee stood up, too. "Do you need anything from the store, Grandpa?" Dee asked. "Or do you want us to do a laundry for you, or—"

"Go look at the pictures," Grandpa said. "Go!"

"It's just terrible," Dee said in a low voice as they moved out of the living room into the hall.

Dezzy sniffed the air. "It smells funny in here," she said.

"Let's look in the kitchen," Dee whispered. "I think it's coming from there."

But nothing looked different in the kitchen. There weren't any dishes in the sink, and when they opened the refrigerator, all the food was neatly arranged inside.

Dezzy kept sniffing the air as they walked upstairs. "What is it?" she asked.

"Maybe it's because the shades are down all over the place," Dee said. She went around pulling up the shades in the upstairs rooms. As the light came through, they could see that everything looked as neat and orderly as usual. In their grandparents' bedroom, the bed was made and nothing was changed. In the closet, where Grandma kept the old photos, her clothes still hung.

It was when they opened the closet and Dezzy sniffed the familiar smell of Grandma's clothes that she knew what had smelled funny all over the house.

"Are you starting in again?" Dee said. "Now what are you crying about?"

"It's because she's dead," Dezzy sobbed. "That's why it smells funny. Because she's not here anymore."

"All right, all right," Dee said angrily, "let's look at pictures."

Another day, Dezzy came over to Grandpa's house by herself. Dee was studying for a math test. She had gotten on the honor roll again with a 3.75 average and decided she wanted to end seventh grade with a 4.0 average. Which meant she needed to raise the B in math to an A. Which was why she was studying.

Dezzy's marks—three Cs, one B minus, and a D— did not get her on the honor roll. Which was why she didn't have to study. Besides, studying made her headaches worse, and even Mom said she shouldn't study if her head ached. "You're getting better all the time anyway," Mom said. "One day, everything will fall into place. Remember—"

"Einstein," Dezzy murmured.

Grandpa opened the door, blinking and scowling. Dezzy could hear the TV. She followed Grandpa into the living room and sat down next to him. Grandpa was watching another baseball game, and when the commercial break came on, he turned to Dezzy and said, "Don't you have someplace to go?"

"No, Grandpa," Dezzy said.

"Where's your sister?"

"She's home studying."

"Well, why aren't you studying, too?" Grandpa sounded cranky.

"Because I didn't get on the honor roll. Dee got on the honor roll, and she wants to raise her marks even higher. I get headaches when I study."

"I used to get headaches, too," Grandpa said.

"And it doesn't do any good anyway," Dezzy told him. "I have a learning disability. That's what Mom says. Dee says I'm just stupid."

The game came on again, and Grandpa resumed watching. Dezzy sat there quietly next to him, watching the game on TV, and not really watching. Not especially doing anything or thinking anything, but feeling comfortable, sitting there in the darkened room with her grandfather.

"She said I was stupid, too," Grandpa said, his eyes still on the set.

"Who said you were stupid, Grandpa?" Dezzy looked up into Grandpa's old face with the TV lights playing on it.

"She did—your grandmother. She said it all the time."

"She said a lot of people were stupid, Grandpa."

"She thought she knew everything. Ha!" Grandpa laughed, but it wasn't a real laugh. "She thought if she ate all that rabbit food, she was going to live forever, and she kept telling me that I was killing myself, and I was stupid, and I . . ."

Here, Grandpa stopped talking and made a terrible choky noise. Tears began rolling down his face, and Dezzy took his hand and cried along with him.

Another day, Grandpa said, "Well, even if you don't study, isn't there something else you like to do?"

"I like to jog, and lots of times I wait for Dad in

the afternoons, but he's tied up now because it's still the tax season. In a few more weeks, he'll be free, but now I don't have anybody to go with, and Mom won't let me go by myself in the park."

"Absolutely not!" Grandpa said. "A girl shouldn't go by herself in the park."

"What about a boy, Grandpa?"

Grandpa had a bowl of Chee-tos on the coffee table in front of the TV. He reached out, took a handful, and said, "It's different for a boy."

"A boy can get robbed, too, Grandpa, or kidnapped, or raped." Dezzy didn't know all the details about rape, but she knew that it could happen to boys as well as girls.

"Talk to your mother," Grandpa said in a cranky voice, and put some more Chee-tos into his mouth. "Just don't go in the park by yourself."

"Grandma used to jog with me sometimes," Dezzy said.

"A lot of good it did her!" Grandpa snorted.

After they sat there together without talking for a while, Grandpa suddenly stood up, walked over to the TV, and turned it off. There were a couple of players on base with only one out, so Dezzy looked up at him in surprise.

"Come on," he said to her. "Let's go."

"Where, Grandpa?"

"To the park. I'll take you jogging."

"But, Grandpa, you never jogged before. You don't even have a sweat suit."

"Are you crazy?" Grandpa said. "I wouldn't be caught dead jogging. I'll just follow along after you in the car."

Every afternoon for the rest of April, Grandpa drove his car along with Dezzy as she jogged in the park.

"It's a miracle," Dad said. "That man hasn't been in the park since before I was born."

"How did you ever get him to come out, Dezzy?" Mom wanted to know. "What did you say?"

"I don't know," Dezzy answered. "Nothing special. Just that I used to go with Dad, and that he was tied up because of the tax season."

"You probably cried all over him," Dee said. "You probably told him you were miserable, and nobody wanted to play with you because you're so weird."

"Now you stop that, Dee!" Mom said sharply. "Why do you always have to make fun of Dezzy? She doesn't make fun of you. And especially now, when she's really accomplished the impossible."

"It's not fair," Dee shouted. "It's just not fair." Then she ran out of the room and slammed the door behind her.

"What's not fair?" Dezzy asked.

Grandpa wasn't used to the park. He wasn't used to all the joggers and the people with dogs, bikes, and babies. He also wasn't used to being honked at so much by other drivers who did not appreciate how slowly Grandpa drove keeping up with Dezzy.

When Grandma was alive, she was the one who yelled and argued, while Grandpa stayed quiet or muttered under his breath. Everything changed when Grandpa came out into the park. He became more like Grandma.

"Oh, yeah!" Grandpa started shouting out his window to other drivers who honked at him. "You know what you can do with that horn!" Sometimes he leaned on his own horn and got into a horn-blasting contest with other drivers. Sometimes he even got out of his car to yell at somebody.

Like the day two boys on bikes stopped Dezzy to ask for directions to the tennis courts. First Grandpa leaned on his horn, and then, since the boys didn't seem to notice, he stopped the car, jumped out, and began shouting, "Get away from her! You stop bothering her or I'll fix you good!"

"You have to go back in the other direction and turn when you pass the big hothouse," Dezzy was saying.

"Oh . . . never mind," said one of the boys, watching Grandpa advance with his fists clenched.

"Thanks very much," said the other, leaping on his bike and racing off, followed by his friend.

Grandpa's eyes were blazing when he reached her.

"It's okay, Grandpa," Dezzy said. "They only wanted to know where the tennis courts were."

"That's what they said," Grandpa snorted. "You just don't talk to any strangers. You hear?"

"Well, okay, Grandpa, but—"

"You just listen to me," Grandpa continued. "It's a good thing I'm with you."

Another day when Dezzy was jogging, Dad's friend Ron and his son Joey came along from the opposite direction. "Hi, Dezzy," Joey yelled out, and stopped.

"Keep going, Joey," his father shouted. "Don't stop."

Joey's face turned sulky. "I will so stop. I want to talk to Dezzy."

"You'll do anything not to jog," said Ron, but he stopped, too.

"You get away from her," Grandpa shouted from the car. He leaned on his horn.

"What's that?" Ron shouted back. "What did you just say, mister?"

"I said you leave her alone or I'll break your neck."

"Who do you think you are?" Ron shouted, advancing toward the car as Grandpa slammed on his brakes.

"Oh, please!" Dezzy ran after Ron. "It's my grandfather."

Grandpa jumped out of the car and approached, his face red, his eyes fierce, his fists clenched.

"Your what?" Ron shook his head.

"Grandpa! Stop, Grandpa!" Dezzy ran in front of him. "This is a friend of Daddy's, and his son, Joey, goes to my school."

"Well, why didn't he say so?" Grandpa said, but he stopped and unclenched his fists.

"Are you . . . Mickey's father?" Ron asked.

"I am. Who are you?"

"I'm Ron Carter. I went to school with Mickey. Saint Ignatius. My mother was friends with your wife."

Grandpa shrugged his shoulders.

"I'm really very sorry, Mr. Ryan, for your loss. She was a wonderful woman. I remember how she used to drive all of us kids to the track meets when we were in school. Mickey used to be a great runner, and my oldest boy . . ."

Ron kept on talking to Grandpa, while other drivers honked because Grandpa had stopped his car without pulling over.

"How come your grandfather is with you and not your father?" Joey asked Dezzy.

"It's the tax season," Dezzy told him, "so my father doesn't have the time."

"I wish my father didn't have the time," Joey said. He looked over at Grandpa and asked in a low voice, "Does he follow after you in the car while you're jogging?"

"Uh-huh. He's not interested in jogging. He just stays inside his car and follows me. Sometimes he gets into fights with other people."

Joey began grinning. "Listen, I have an idea.

Would it be okay with you if I came out jogging with you and your grandfather? Maybe I wouldn't have to go with my father if I could go with you."

"That man's a jerk," Grandpa said after Ron and Joey left.

"That's what Dad said," Dezzy told him.

"He kept telling me that his boy, the one who was talking to you, doesn't measure up to his brother. That he has weak ankles, and he has to drag him out jogging, and that the kid doesn't want to go. What kind of crazy country is this anyway?"

"Joey wants to come jogging with us," Dezzy said. "I told him I'd ask you if it was okay."

"It's okay," Grandpa said, "but I'm not going to make him jog if he doesn't want to. I don't care what's wrong with his ankles. And if that man thinks I'm going to force his kid to do anything he doesn't want to do, he's got another think coming."

But, as it turned out, Grandpa didn't have to force Joey to do anything he didn't want to do. Joey only wanted to sit in the car with Grandpa and lean on the horn and shout things out the window while Dezzy jogged along by herself.

When the tax season ended, early in May, Dad resumed jogging in the afternoons. But he asked Dezzy not to come with him.

"Just pretend it's still the tax season, and I'm not jogging afternoons. I'll go out to the beach so I don't bump into you."

"But I love going with you," Dezzy protested. "Sometimes we talk things over, and I never have to break up any fights when I'm with you."

"I know, Dezzy," Dad said. "But it's really wonderful for Grandpa. It gets him out of the house and gives him a sense of importance."

"Well, maybe he could keep on driving along with the two of us."

"He'd never agree to that. And, Dezzy, it's good for Joey, too. His father was telling me the other day that Joey's ankles seem to have strengthened, and his muscle tone has improved since he's been jogging with you."

"But, Dad, he doesn't jog with me. He stays in the car with Grandpa, and the two of them get into fights with people."

Finally Dad and Dezzy agreed to a compromise. Dezzy would continue to go jogging afternoons with Grandpa, but she could also jog with Dad any morning she was up early enough. Maybe he didn't think she would be able to get up at six or six-thirty, but she did.

Mr. Franklin, Dezzy's science teacher, asked her to stay after class.

"I don't know what we can do, Dezzy," Mr. Franklin said, "but I'm afraid you're going to fail science unless you can really work a little harder."

"I try, Mr. Franklin," Dezzy said, "but I have a learning disability, and—"

"I know all about your learning disability," Mr. Franklin said, "but you haven't been doing your homework, and you never picked a topic for your science project. It's due before the end of the term."

"I can't think of anything that interests me." Dezzy's eyes filled with tears. "I try, Mr. Franklin, but I guess I just don't like science. It's boring."

Mr. Franklin looked unhappy. He was a kind man, a patient man, and one of those teachers who didn't enjoy seeing students cry.

"Everything in life has to do with science," Mr. Franklin said earnestly.

Dezzy shook her head. Her nose began running, and she fished around inside her pocket for a tissue.

"Some people enjoy collecting rocks . . . or shells . . . or flowers," Mr. Franklin said desperately. "It's all right with me if students just bring in collections of things with a few labels."

"I'm not interested in rocks or shells or flowers," Dezzy said sadly. The tears were running down her face, and Mr. Franklin began nervously shuffling around some papers on his desk.

● ● ●

Dad and Dezzy were jogging along Ocean Beach on a brilliant sunny morning. The sky was blue, the water sparkled, and other brightly dressed people in red, blue, and purple sweat suits ran along with them at the water's edge. A perfect day—but not quite perfect, because one dead sea gull lay on a heap of broken glass bottles and a pile of garbage.

Dezzy stopped running, and Dad did, too.

"It's disgusting," Dad said angrily, "how people foul up this beautiful world."

Dezzy looked around the beach where they were standing. It was littered with broken bottles, plastic bags, balloons, straws, and bits and pieces of food.

"It looks like people had a big party," Dezzy said, "and forgot to clean up their garbage."

"And just look at that poor bird!" Dad said. "It must have eaten some of the junk."

They started running again, and Dezzy asked, "Did Grandma die because of what she ate?"

"No, Dezzy, you know Grandma died because of a stroke—a clot in her brain. It had nothing to do with what she ate. It couldn't have been prevented. I guess her time had just come."

Dad stopped talking, and Dezzy did, too.

But on another morning, she picked up the conversation where it had left off. It was a cold, foggy morning, and not as many people were out jogging. The beach, Dezzy noticed, was littered with plastic bags, cups, six-pack rings, and pieces of food. No dead bird lay on the ground, but Dezzy was still thinking of the one she'd seen with Dad.

"Do you think that bird died because it ate people's garbage?" Dezzy asked.

"What bird?"

"The dead bird we saw a few days ago on the beach."

"Yes, I'm pretty sure it did," Dad said. "Human junk food isn't good for humans, much less birds."

"Then Grandma was right," Dezzy said.

"Well, yes, I guess so," Dad agreed. "But if people would only take care of their garbage properly, and not throw it around, at least we wouldn't have to worry about killing birds and animals."

"Maybe if all of us picked up garbage, we'd save the birds."

"Nobody likes to clean up other people's messes," Dad said. "Everybody has to clean up his or her own.

Anyway, Dezzy, look at that boat out there. Isn't it a beauty?"

There was garbage all over the school yard. Dezzy saw a couple of blackbirds perched on some candy-bar wrappers, and she ran at them and chased them away.

"Dezzy, will you stop acting like a baby," Dee cried out. Dee was sitting on a bench with Megan and some of her friends.

"I don't want any birds to die," Dezzy said. She bent down, picked up the candy-bar wrappers, and threw them into the garbage can.

"How about garbage?" Dezzy smiled up into Mr. Franklin's puzzled face.

"Garbage?"

"How about garbage and birds? How about how garbage kills birds, and how we should do something about it?"

"Ah . . ." Now Mr. Franklin was smiling, too. "Waste management," he said happily. "That is a very important subject in the control of pollution. Yes, that would be an excellent subject for a science project. But, Dezzy, how are you going to approach it?"

"I'm going to pick it up," she told him.

Grandpa said he wanted to take Dezzy and Joey to the penny arcade over at the beach.

"I used to go there when I was a kid, and I used to take my own kids."

"Hey, that's great," Joey said. "I've gone a couple of times, and I love it."

"They have some of the old machines, from the turn of the century," Grandpa said. "I used to like the gypsy fortune-teller. You put in a penny, and you watch her move her fingers over the cards, and then one comes out for you. And there's a baseball game where you have to play against somebody else, and there are some old silent movies—"

"And there's 'Pac-Man' and 'Street Fighter,'" Joey added.

Grandpa gave each of them two dollars but said they could have more if they needed it. He was surprised that everything cost at least twenty-five cents or fifty cents. But he played one of the player pianos for them and showed them a funny old exhibit of a carnival.

Everything was made of toothpicks, from the Ferris wheel to the roller coaster to the bandstand. When you put a quarter in, the Ferris wheel started turning, the band began to play, and all the little toothpick machines moved one way or another. Grandpa really enjoyed himself. He made the three of them pose for pictures at the picture machine. It cost a dollar fifty, but they got a strip of four pictures with all of them grinning and sticking out their tongues.

Joey said he wanted to play the computer games. He took them to the back of the arcade, where all the computer games were flashing and making loud noises. Grandpa said he didn't think he'd enjoy playing a computer game, but Joey got him to try. He, Joey, and Dezzy played "Race Driving" and "Star Wars." Then Grandpa got some more change, and the three of them played "Terminator" and "Street Fighter."

Finally Dezzy got bored. Grandpa and Joey were now playing "Judgment Day" and yelling "Pow" and "Zap" and "Crunch." She wandered up and down the aisles, looking at some of the old machines and listening to the player piano. Finally she walked outside onto the walk above the ocean. She picked up a cigarette wrapper and a couple of cigarette butts and tossed them into the garbage can. Then she stood at the wall overlooking the water. She could hear the sounds of the seals barking from Seal Rock, and she watched the cormorants circling and diving for fish.

For the first time since Grandma died, she really felt completely happy.

How is your project coming along?" Mr. Franklin asked Dezzy.

Dezzy said happily, "I clean up the school yard every day after lunch, and I keep chasing away the birds from anything that they might choke on. When I go jogging in the afternoons now, I take along some bags and pick up garbage in the park. I'd like to take along bags when I go jogging with my father on the beach, only"—Dezzy's face fell—"he doesn't like me to pick up other people's garbage."

Mr. Franklin said, "Well, it certainly sounds as if you're doing your bit to clean up the environment, and I am impressed. But, Dezzy, how are you working this into your project?"

"That is my project," Dezzy said. "Cleaning up the place and saving the birds."

"I think you need to do more," Mr. Franklin said gently. "You need to show how garbage has an adverse effect on animals, on streams, maybe on the air we breathe. You might want to talk about the oil slick that killed so many birds and fish up in Alaska a few years ago. Some garbage isn't even biodegradable. You know how serious a problem that is."

Dezzy didn't know. She also didn't know what *biodegradable* meant.

"Look it up in a book on recycling, Dezzy," Mr. Franklin said, trying not to notice Dezzy's puzzled face. "A reference book will help you organize your report."

Dezzy wanted to tell him that she didn't think it would and that most likely it would simply give her a headache like other books. But she restrained herself.

One day Joey found a ten-dollar bill. Somebody had thrown a couple of banana peels, one half-eaten chocolate doughnut, a piece of a hot dog in a bun, three napkins, seven plastic cups, four plastic plates, one broken plastic fork, and two broken plastic spoons right in front of the statue of Francis Scott Key in the park. Dezzy was picking them up. Joey was trying to get Dezzy to resume jogging so he and her grandfather could also resume cruising along behind her.

"What I can't figure out," Dezzy said, "was what happened to the other forks and spoons."

"Come on, Dezzy," Joey pleaded, "let's get going."

"I mean, if you have seven plastic cups and four plastic plates, how come there are only two spoons and one fork? Doesn't that mean the people threw some of their garbage away? Why do you think they didn't throw all of it away?" Dezzy picked everything up off the ground, put it into a bag, and headed for the garbage can.

"I don't know, Dezzy, but let's get going. Please! Your grandfather is falling asleep."

He followed her to the garbage can, and while he was standing over it, just before Dezzy tossed in her sack of garbage, he noticed the ten-dollar bill. It was in an open bag with a couple of beer cans partially covering it.

Joey offered to split the ten dollars with her, but

Dezzy told him she didn't want it. After that, Joey began helping Dezzy collect garbage, too. He brought along his own bags, but he never found another ten-dollar bill. He did find a slightly used San Francisco Giants cap, a new harmonica, three quarters, five dimes, lots of pennies, and one ladies' gold chain. He offered the chain to Dezzy, and she took it.

Dezzy never found anything special, but Joey said it was because she didn't know how to look. Grandpa didn't mind parking while they collected garbage. Sometimes he listened to a ball game, sometimes he took a nap, and sometimes he argued with different policemen who told him he was parked in a restricted zone.

One Saturday morning, after Dezzy had returned from jogging with Dad and was wondering whether she should 1) go to the library and try to find a book about garbage, 2) watch some TV, 3) drop in on Grandpa, or 4) call Rachel Castori and find out what she was doing, Dee came into her room and asked, "Do you want to come to the mall with me, Dezzy?"

Dezzy looked at her sister in surprise.

"It was Mom's idea," Dee said in a sour voice. "All my friends are busy today, and Mom said I couldn't go to the mall unless you came with me."

"Oh!" said Dezzy.

"Well?"

"What are you going to do there?" Dezzy wanted to know.

"I'm going to do what I always do there," Dee snapped. "You really do ask dumb questions, Dezzy."

"No, I don't think I want to go," Dezzy said.

"Well, all right for you!" Dee turned around, and Dezzy resumed her deliberations. She really should go to the library and find a book about garbage, she thought, and immediately her head began aching. Maybe if Rachel was free, she could go with her.

Dee turned around again. "What are you doing that's so important anyway?"

"I need to go to the library," Dezzy said.

"The library?" Dee's eyes opened very wide.

"It's for my science project. Mr. Franklin thinks I should get a book about garbage."

"You know, you really are weird, Dezzy." Dee smiled her mean smile, and Dezzy's eyes began filling with tears.

"Okay, never mind," Dee said quickly. "I'll tell you what—if you come to the mall with me, I'll go to the library with you."

Dezzy sniffed back her tears. "It's a deal," she said.

They had fun. They ate candy. Dezzy threw away the wrappers in a garbage can and picked up some other candy wrappers she noticed on the ground even though she didn't have to worry about birds in the mall. Dee bought earrings for herself—little star-shaped posts with tiny blue stones in the center. And suddenly Dezzy wanted earrings, too. Both had had their ears pierced when they turned twelve, but most of the time Dezzy just wore her old gold posts and forgot she was wearing them. Today she wanted a new pair so badly that Dee had to restrain her from just buying the first pair she tried on.

"What's the big hurry?" Dee laughed. She was in great spirits. "You hardly ever know what you're wearing anyway."

"Oh, those are so beautiful," Dezzy said, pointing to a pair of twisted gold-colored wires with small red beads.

"How about this pair?" Dee showed her white heart-shaped earrings.

"Oh, they're beautiful, too, and—oh, look, Dee, at those blue-and-silver spangly ones."

Finally Dezzy picked out a pair of big white daisy posts with yellow centers. Her hands shook as she put them on. She couldn't wait to see herself in her new earrings.

She moved her head around this way and that way in front of the mirror.

"You look just like Mom when you do that," Dee said.

"I do?"

"She's always moving her head around and tossing her hair like she's got some in her eyes even though she doesn't. Keep your head still!"

Dezzy kept her head still and looked at the girl with daisy earrings, smiling back at her from the mirror. She looked at herself for a long time.

"I look nice," she said. "Don't I, Dee?"

Dee didn't answer. By this time, she was busy looking at herself again in another mirror. Later they wandered around the mall, giggling together like they used to do about how funny other people looked.

At the poster store, Dee bought herself a poster of
a rock band while Dezzy bought herself a poster of a
clean sandy beach with a deep, deep blue sky over-
head and snowy white sea gulls flying in and out of
bright green words that said SAVE OUR EARTH.

Other people at Dezzy's school picked up garbage in the school yard during lunch as well as Dezzy. They didn't want to pick up garbage. They had to.

"You don't have to bother, Dezzy," said Ms. Finkelstein, the vice-principal, who was in charge of lockers, latecomers, litterers, and people who had to pick up garbage because of lateness, littering, or other assorted discipline problems. She motioned to a large group of surly-looking students who were picking up lunch debris.

"They don't do a good job," Dezzy said critically.

"They leave straws all over the place, and birds can choke on straws."

Ms. Finkelstein turned her attention to a boy who had carelessly tossed some garbage into a can, strewing a good part of it onto the ground. "Get back there, Tony," she yelled. "You're making more of a mess there than before you started cleaning up."

"I think we should only let people clean up the yard who want to," Dezzy said.

"If we waited for volunteers," Ms. Finkelstein replied, "we'd never get it cleaned up."

"There's another weirdo in my English class just like you," Dee told Dezzy. "His name is Lenny Gee. We all had to write a poem, and he wrote one about how the world was going to die because of garbage and pollution. It was the most boring thing I ever heard in my life."

Dezzy's written report on garbage was returned to her with a C minus.

"I'm sorry, Dezzy," Mr. Franklin said, "but it seems to me you copied most of it from a book."

"Well, yes, I did," Dezzy said, "I did copy most of

it from the book I took out of the library. You said I should get a book."

"Yes, I did say you should get a book, but, Dezzy, you know you're not supposed to copy the information right out of it. You know you're supposed to put it into your own words."

"Well, the book says it better than I can," Dezzy told him. "And besides, I'm more interested in doing something about it than writing a report."

Mr. Franklin said, "Well, Dezzy, at least you're not going to fail, but I really don't think I can give you a higher mark than C minus."

"That's fine," Dezzy told him. "If you give me a C minus, then I won't have any Ds this term. That's pretty good for me."

"You can do a lot better than that, Dezzy," Mr. Franklin said earnestly. "Don't be discouraged. Lots of people overcome problems, and one day—"

"I know," Dezzy murmured. "His name was Einstein."

"I keep telling you not to bother, Dezzy," Ms. Finkelstein said another day. She motioned angrily to two girls who were talking to each other. "Lisa Falladi and Sara Tuchman—you're not here to chat.

Just start picking up all that junk over there near the gate."

Dezzy watched as the girls slowly sauntered off in the direction of the garbage. "They're not interested," she said severely.

"Well, I guess most people aren't," said Ms. Finkelstein. "That's why we had to set this up as a punishment."

"I think there are people who would like to do it," Dezzy insisted. "There's a boy in my sister's class who wrote a poem about pollution and garbage, and my friend Joey told me he knows a girl named Amanda Fonzi who just transferred from a school that had a recycling club."

"I don't think it would work here," said Ms. Finkelstein.

"How do we know if we don't try?" Dezzy said.

"All right. Come talk to me one day after school," Ms. Finkelstein agreed as she darted off to intercept a boy who was about to slip a banana peel down another boy's shirt.

Joey found a number of interesting things in the park's garbage. Some he passed on to Dezzy and some to Grandpa. He gave Grandpa a book of sports crossword puzzles and an unused bag of charcoal. Joey also found a leather wallet with nothing inside, which he kept; a small red backpack, which he gave to Dezzy; and lots of tubes of suntan lotion, which nobody wanted. Sometimes Dezzy wore the gold chain Joey had given her. It looked good with her new daisy earrings.

"Ms. Finkelstein said we could start a recycling club at school next term," Dezzy told Joey one day while they were collecting garbage around the fly-casting pools in the park. "I went and talked to her yesterday. She doesn't think many kids would want to join, but she said we could try."

"Hey, Dezzy," Joey yelled as he pulled something out of a garbage can, "look at this!" He held up a pair of men's gloves.

"Are they for different hands?" Dezzy wanted to know.

"Yes, but the thumb is torn on one of them." Joey pulled them on. "I think they're leather, but they're too big for me. Do you think your grandfather would want them?"

"I don't know, Joey, but anyway, I told Ms. Finkelstein that I was going to ask you to join."

Joey shook his head and waggled the big gloves at her. "It wouldn't be any fun at school," he said. "You'd have to return everything you found, and you'd have Ms. Finkelstein bossing you around."

"I told her maybe we could even move out into the neighborhood. Maybe you wouldn't have to return everything you found out on the streets. But, Joey, that's not really why we're collecting garbage, is it?"

"Oh, no, of course not," Joey said as he looked carefully through a pile of newspapers before dropping them into the can.

Mom and Dad didn't let Dee fill out the application for Camp Cornell until the end of May.

"It's probably going to be too late," Dee grumbled. "This camp fills up quickly. That's what Lori Ferguson's cousin said."

"Any camp that costs so much," Dad said, "will probably have lots of vacancies."

"But we'll manage," Mom added. She looked at Dezzy. "What do you say, Dezzy? Wouldn't you like to go, too? It really won't be a problem if you want to go, too."

"I don't want to go," Dezzy said. "I'm not interested in acting. I want to go to Camp Sierra."

"You don't have to act," Dee said. "They have other activities."

"Like what?"

"Like painting and drawing."

"I'm not interested in painting and drawing."

"And ceramics."

"I'm not interested in ceramics."

"They have singing and dancing, too. Come on, Dezzy, you love singing and dancing."

"I do?"

"Maybe you could be in the chorus or even do a dance solo in a musical."

"No," Dezzy said slowly, "I'm not interested in—"

"You're not interested in anything," Dee shouted.

"Yes, I am," Dezzy protested.

"Like what?"

"Well, I like to jog, and I—"

"What?"

"I . . ." Dezzy felt her eyes beginning to fill up.

"You're not interested in anything," Dee cried. "Other people have hobbies, but all you do is go around picking up garbage. It's disgusting."

"Yes, it is," Dezzy agreed. "It is disgusting how people throw their garbage all over the place."

Joey was going to Boston for the summer. That's where his mother lived. Under the divorce agreement, Joey and his brother stayed with their mother during the Christmas, Easter, and summer vacations.

"How come you live with your dad if you can't stand him?" Dezzy wanted to know.

Joey shrugged his shoulders but didn't answer.

Dezzy thought she probably should stop asking questions, but if the question continued in her own mind, she never could stop herself.

"Didn't your mother want you to stay with her?" she asked.

Joey looked down at the ground. "No, she didn't," he said.

"That's terrible!" Dezzy wondered what it would feel like if one of her parents didn't want her. It would feel like death—like a bird choking on a straw. Dezzy started crying, noisily.

"Cut it out!" Joey said angrily. "We're better off without her. She never let anybody be. My father's a pain, but at least he's not around all the time.

She was always around and always wanted us to be doing something we didn't want to be doing or to be going somewhere we didn't want to go or . . ." Joey's voice faded out.

"Well, do you have fun when you spend the summers with her?"

"She's working now," Joey said, "so she's not home a lot, and my brother and I are old enough to be on our own. He goes off with his friends there, so I'm not stuck with him either. I can take care of myself."

"It doesn't sound like much fun," Dezzy said.

Joey kept looking down at the ground. "It's more fun hanging out with you and your grandfather," he said.

Dezzy wanted to say something to cheer him up. Nobody was making her go anywhere she didn't want to go.

"Maybe I'll . . . maybe Grandpa and I will write you a letter," she said.

Joey looked up and smiled. "Okay," he said, "and maybe I'll write you one. Maybe I'll even check out the garbage in Boston and send you some."

Joey was the first to go—as soon as school ended. Dee left right after the July Fourth holiday. The next day she called from Camp Cornell. She wanted to come home. First she talked to Mom and cried that she was homesick and that she didn't like any of the girls in her bunk and that she wanted to leave right away.

Dezzy wanted to talk to her, but Dee said she didn't want to talk to Dezzy.

So Dad got on the phone and talked and talked and talked. Finally he got Dee to agree that she would stay one more night at Camp Cornell, and that if she still felt the same way the next day, she could come home.

"And we'd lose a whole week's deposit," Dad grumbled. But not to Dee. He said it to Mom and Dezzy after he hung up.

"It must be a terrible camp," Dezzy said. "Dee was never homesick at Camp Sierra."

"It's not that," Mom said. "It's because you're not there. She's not used to going away to camp without you."

"But she said she didn't want to talk to me," Dezzy said. "I thought she was angry with me."

"She is, darling," Mom said, "because she really misses you so much. I know Dee talks tough sometimes, but she's really pretty tender inside. Not like you."

"What do you mean not like me?" Dezzy demanded. Her eyes flooded, and her nose began running. "I'm the one who cries all the time, and Dee makes fun of me and says I'm a weirdo."

"Well, yes, I know," Mom said, "but it takes courage to be a . . . no . . . I mean . . . it takes courage to be different. Kids your age all want to be the same. Dee isn't as brave as you."

Dezzy wasn't feeling very brave. She was feeling Dee's loneliness, and her own loneliness.

"I want her to come home," she sobbed. "I want her to come home right away."

"It's not easy being a parent," Dad sighed. But he pulled Dezzy onto his lap and patted her back.

The next day Dee was feeling better. She was even willing to talk to Dezzy.

"They said I could have a small part in the first play," she said, "and I could learn how to do makeup. And then maybe I'll have a bigger part in the second play. Marcia—that's the drama coach—says she thinks I have a lot of natural poise."

Dezzy wanted to say, "Come home, Dee—right away! Come home, and we'll both go to Camp Sierra and have fun like we always do." She was missing Dee a lot, but as Dee kept on talking about the girls in her own bunk and the cute boys in another bunk, Dezzy just sniffled quietly to herself and shut up.

Dezzy was supposed to leave for Camp Sierra on Sunday, July 19. On the Friday before, she fractured her ankle. It happened while she was jogging in the park with Grandpa cruising behind her. She heard a crash, thought something had happened to Grandpa's car, turned to look, twisted her foot on a curb, and ended up on the ground with her ankle hurting in a way it had never hurt before.

The crash didn't have anything to do with Grandpa. It was caused by some furniture falling out of a U-Haul.

Grandpa stayed cool. He checked her ankle and said right away that he thought it was broken. He said he could tell because he had broken his ankle once when he fell down a flight of stairs. It looked just the way Dezzy's ankle looked. Grandpa said he guessed Dezzy and he had a lot in common.

Dezzy started crying as soon as she tried to stand and felt the pain shooting all the way up her leg. Grandpa stayed cool. He told her not to worry. They'd go to the hospital right away, and if there was one thing those idiot doctors could do these days, it was fix broken bones. He assured her she'd be fine.

Dezzy cried all the way to the hospital and while they were in the waiting room waiting for the doctor. Grandpa stayed cool. He bought her a Coke, some corn chips, and a candy bar, but she was too busy crying to eat or drink anything. Grandpa said she'd feel a lot better after she saw the doctor. He ate the corn chips and candy bar and drank the Coke.

Dezzy didn't feel better after she saw the doctor. It hurt her even more after he put the cast on. But she did stop crying because suddenly she noticed Grandpa's eyes and cheeks wet with tears.

"It's okay, Grandpa. I'm going to stop crying now," she told him. "It's okay."

It really wasn't okay. To begin with, Dezzy couldn't go to Camp Sierra, because of her fractured ankle.

And then there were all the whispered conversations between Mom and Dad. They were supposed to be leaving for a week's cruise to Alaska in a couple of days.

"We can always go another time, darling," Mom said brightly. "We don't mind a bit staying home and hanging out with you. Do we, Mickey?"

"Oh! No . . . no . . . of course not," Dad said glumly.

"Are you going to lose your deposit, Dad?" Dezzy asked sympathetically.

"Only part of it."

"Mickey!" Mom shook her head and smiled at Dezzy. "That's not important, Dezzy. We'll all have fun. We'll plan some outings. Maybe we'll see some good movies and eat in some nice restaurants. We'll have fun, won't we, Mickey?"

"Oh? Sure . . . sure."

Dezzy knew that Mom and Dad always looked forward to the summers. Usually they planned a vacation for just the two of them while the girls were away at camp. In the past, both Dezzy and Dee had resented the vacations their parents took without them. The girls had resented the photos Mom and Dad took showing them having fun by themselves. They resented the mementos their parents brought back, and the memories that did not include them. But since Dee was already away enjoying herself without Dezzy, it didn't seem so important if Mom and Dad did the same.

"Why don't you both go on the cruise?" Dezzy said. "It's only for a week."

"Out of the question," Mom said. "We're staying home with you."

"I can stay with Grandpa," Dezzy suggested.

"I wouldn't think of it," Mom said.

"I wonder if he would," said Dad.

C H A P T E R

Dezzy slept in Dad's old room. Not much had been changed since he was a boy. Pennants from different baseball and football teams hung on the walls, and all Dad's sports trophies were arranged in rows on chests and bookcases around the room.

There was a large framed picture of Dad in a cap and gown from when he graduated from high school. Dad was smiling in that photo, and he was also smiling in another large framed picture of himself in a different cap and gown from when he graduated from college.

Other photos of Dad—in running shorts, on track teams, with his brother and sister or parents or his whole original family—also hung on the walls. There were no pictures of him with Mom or with Dee and Dezzy.

Every morning during the week her parents were away, Dezzy woke up to those pictures of Dad from before he was a dad. She also woke up to the sounds of Grandpa trying to go down the stairs quietly. One of the steps creaked and Grandpa wheezed, and sometimes it was the creak that woke Dezzy up and sometimes it was Grandpa's wheeze as he tried to get down the stairs without the creak happening. Those mornings, Dezzy lay very still, waiting for the creak and then waiting for Grandpa to stop. She knew Grandpa didn't want to wake her and was standing there on the step, listening to see if he had. Dezzy tried to stay very quiet, hardly breathing, until she heard him move on.

Once he was downstairs, Grandpa quietly left the house. Dezzy knew he would be back with fresh doughnuts or cinnamon bread. At home, Dezzy generally just had some orange juice and a bowl of Cheerios for breakfast. But Grandpa's cheeks always looked so rosy and his eyes so bright that she tried to act really happy over his breakfast offerings.

"They've been making this cinnamon bread ever since we first moved in here," Grandpa told her. "First it was Old Man Schumann, and now it's his boy Chas." Grandpa laughed. "He's not really a boy anymore. He's close to my age, and his daughter, Marge, she's really running the place these days."

"Delicious, Grandpa," Dezzy said, trying to look enthusiastic. Grandpa was always disappointed that she didn't want any eggs and bacon.

"Take another piece, Dezzy," Grandpa urged. "You could use a little extra meat on your bones."

Mom had left all kinds of food in Grandpa's freezer. There were frozen meat loaves, frozen chicken cacciatore, frozen lasagna, and frozen chili. Mom had also bought steaks, chops, and one canned ham. Grandpa told her not to, but she insisted.

"She can take it all back when they come home," Grandpa said.

"But, Grandpa, it would save you a lot of work," Dezzy told him. "And she's a good cook. Even you say she is."

"She is," Grandpa agreed. "But I like my own cooking best."

Grandpa liked shopping, too. Everybody seemed to know him. Even in the big stores.

"How are you, Mr. Ryan?"

"Fine, Joe, fine. You got any of your special horse meat for me today?"

"That's a good one, Mr. Ryan. You're certainly some joker, you are."

"Ha-ha-ha!"

Grandpa was a different man when he was shopping from the way he was out cruising in the park. He smiled and joked around a lot. People really seemed to know him.

"That your granddaughter, Mr. Ryan?"

"Yup. That's my little Dezzy. Broke her leg so she could stay with her old grandpa while the rest of the family went away on vacation."

"Can't say I blame her, Mr. Ryan."

"Ha-ha-ha-ha!"

Sometimes Dezzy stayed home when Grandpa went shopping. It was embarrassing to hear how friendly and hearty he was. Not that she preferred him nasty, the way he often was in the park. Not exactly—but he didn't seem so silly when he was nasty.

A couple of times, Grandpa took her out to dinner. Dezzy always liked going out to dinner. One time they went out to a steak house and ate steak and french fries. Another time Grandpa said she could pick the restaurant.

"How about a salad bar?" Dezzy suggested.

"A salad bar?" Grandpa said things like "Yuck" and "Barf," but he took her anyway.

"This isn't bad," he said as he followed her around. Dezzy was hobbling without crutches by now. The salad bar included fried chicken, spaghetti, Jell-O, and three desserts with whipped cream. Grandpa went back three times and managed to skip all the vegetables and salads entirely.

Every morning they went out cruising.

"It will be about two months, the doctor thought, before I can jog again," Dezzy said longingly.

Now that the summer vacation had started, there were many more people in the park and more garbage scattered all over the place. One day Dezzy became so depressed that Grandpa suggested they go someplace else. He drove Dezzy over the Golden Gate Bridge into Sausalito. The weather changed from cold and foggy in the city to warm and sunny in Sausalito. The garbage also changed.

"Grandpa, how come there's less garbage on the streets? It's so much cleaner here."

"It's because a lot of rich people live here," Grandpa said. He was zooming up and down the hills. The views were spectacular, and so were the clean streets.

"Are rich people neater than poor people?" Dezzy wanted to know. "Do they always throw their garbage away in cans?"

Grandpa snorted. "If you're rich, you can get other people to pick up your garbage."

"That's all right," Dezzy said. "Some people are more interested in cleaning up garbage than other people. But I wouldn't only clean up rich people's garbage. I'd clean up everybody's garbage."

"Everybody should clean up their own," Grandpa said, whipping down a twisty narrow road.

"But they don't," Dezzy said.

"Well, that's what's wrong with the world," Grandpa said in a cranky voice, jerking to a sudden stop in front of a red light. "Anyway, Dezzy, I'm getting hungry. How about some pizza? There's a great pizza place I used to go to."

The pizza place wasn't there anymore. Instead, a fancy coffee shop with lots of gleaming copper machines showed through a large, clean glass window. Clean, shiny-looking people sat around inside, drinking coffee and laughing.

Grandpa muttered nasty things about yuppies, but Dezzy marveled at the clean streets.

"We're going to start a special club at my school in the fall," she told Grandpa, "and we're going to clean up the school yard and maybe the neighborhood. I hope it gets to look like this."

"Just don't let them open a place like that," Grandpa said in disgust.

Afternoons, Grandpa often watched a game on TV. Sometimes Dezzy watched with him. Other times she looked at the old photos or talked on the phone to whoever was available. Rachel Castori was away at music camp, but Dezzy spoke to Rachel's mother and heard about how everybody marveled at Rachel's brilliant playing. Sometimes Dezzy's own parents called. Dezzy also wrote letters to Dee and Rachel, and one to Joey. She said:

> *Dear Joey,*
>
> *I fractured my ankle and can't jog. The doctor says I probably won't for two months. That will be September. After school opens. Otherwise, I am fine. I hope you are fine, too.*
>
> *I am staying with my grandfather. The rest of my family went on vacation. Are you having fun? What is it like in Boston?*
>
> *Grandpa is going to write something, too. I hope you write to us soon.*
>
> > *Your friend,*
> > *Dezzy*

Grandpa added something about how lousy the Boston Red Sox were doing, and how he hoped Joey was doing better than the Red Sox.

Joey wrote back before the week ended. He said he was okay, and he was sorry Dezzy broke her ankle. He also said he had gone to see a Red Sox game with his mother's boyfriend, who was kind of boring but meant well.

> *He thought I'd like to go because it*
> *was my birthday, so he took me and*
> *my brother and my mother. The food*
> *was okay.*
> *I guess you haven't been collecting*
> *garbage since you fractured your ankle.*
> *I have, and I found a picture frame*
> *my mother said she could use and a*
> *brand-new electric razor my brother*
> *says he can use. (Don't believe it.)*
> *I also found a perfectly good nail*
> *clipper, about four dollars in change,*
> *and a surprise for the two of you.*
> *It's coming in the mail.*
>
> > *Your friend,*
> > *Joe*

Grandpa and Dezzy kept checking the mail after Joey's letter, but no package arrived for them. They didn't wait, though, to send him a package for his birthday. Grandpa had an idea. He took Dezzy down

to Fisherman's Wharf to a store he said had the kind
of things they wanted. Only the store wasn't there
anymore. But they did finally find one on Sutter
Street, and they both picked out funny things—a
Groucho Marx mask; a can of what looked like peanuts, only a snake jumped out when you opened it;
a flower that squirted water when you tried to smell
it; a little toy mouse that ran across the floor and
looked real; a little dangling toy spider that also
looked real; a tiny button that made a loud squeak
when you sat on it; a folded handkerchief with a
bloody finger in it. . . . Dezzy had to restrain Grandpa
from buying out the store. As it was, the box they
ended up sending Joey was a pretty big one and
needed a lot of postage.

Dezzy loved looking at the old family photos while she stayed with Grandpa. Some were pasted in albums with pages that cracked when you turned them, and others were just thrown into boxes in Grandpa's closet.

There was a wedding picture of Grandma and Grandpa. Grandma wore a three-quarter-length dress with a tight waist and a scooped neckline. She had a funny hat perched on her head, like a pancake with puffs of veil. She was beautiful—slim and smiling and happy. Sometimes Dezzy kissed the picture of Grandma and cried.

Grandpa wore a uniform, because he was in the army then. He looked very handsome and happy, and a lot like Dad, only heavier. Not that Grandpa was fat then, just heavier than Dad. In later pictures, as their children were born, you could see Grandpa grow fatter and fatter, and begin to lose his hair as he gained weight.

There were pictures of Dad as a child, and Aunt Mary and Uncle Bill, too. There were pictures of cousins, aunts, and uncles whom Dezzy knew. But there were also pictures of people she didn't know. Some of them Grandpa could identify. Others he couldn't.

"That's somebody on your grandma's side," he usually said when he didn't know who the person was.

Some of the other boxes in the closet that Dezzy liked to look through held old letters. She liked to read Dad's letters that he wrote home from camp when he was a boy. There was one that said: *Dear Mom and Dad,* in a funny, kid's handwriting, *I am having fun. Now I can swim good. Don't forget to feed Ralph. Love, Mickey.*

"Who was Ralph?" Dezzy asked Grandpa.

First Grandpa said he didn't remember. Then he

did. Ralph was a turtle—one of many Dad kept when he was a boy. Grandpa said Dad was always bringing animals home—cats, dogs, turtles, even a snake once, which Grandma made him take back to the park.

"That's funny," Dezzy said. "He's not interested in animals anymore."

"Well, he's got a family now," Grandpa answered. But then he shook his head and said, "People change. Everything changes. The longer you live, the more you realize that."

"Did you change much, Grandpa?" Dezzy wanted to know. She was thinking of him in his wedding picture when he was young and handsome and smiling.

"Go away," Grandpa said. "I'm busy."

He was only watching one of his games on TV, but he never liked to answer questions about himself.

On the day before her parents returned home, Dezzy found a picture she had never seen before. It was in a box of old letters, and it was stuck to an envelope down at the bottom. Dezzy managed to detach it and found herself looking at a woman in a large hat with a dead bird on it. The woman looked familiar even though she was wearing an old-fashioned high-necked lacy blouse and a long skirt.

"Who is this?" Dezzy asked Grandpa.

"I don't know," Grandpa said even before he looked at the picture.

"Come on, Grandpa. Take a real look."

The commercial break came on, so Grandpa could focus his attention on the photo.

"I don't know who it is," he said. "Probably somebody on your grandmother's side."

"She's got a dead bird on her hat." Dezzy's voice choked up.

"Now, Dezzy, you stop that," Grandpa said. "That bird's been dead a long time." He laughed. "And so has the lady, whoever she is."

"But why would anybody wear a dead bird on her hat? It's weird."

"Well, maybe that was the fashion then." Grandpa studied the picture. "She really does look familiar, though, doesn't she?"

"But even if it was the fashion, it's still weird. Why should you want to wear a dead bird even if people told you to?"

"People wear fur coats nowadays," Grandpa said.

"Well, I think that's pretty weird, too," Dezzy said.

Grandpa held the picture a little farther away from him. "She really does look familiar. I wonder..."

Dezzy was looking at the picture, too. It came to her whom the woman in the picture looked like. "I know. I know," she shouted. "She looks just like Dee."

"That's it," Grandpa said. The commercial ended and the game started up again, but Grandpa kept looking at the picture. "Maybe," he said, "she's somebody from my side."

"She's pretty," Dezzy said, "but I hate her hat."

"Maybe she was my grandmother. Don't you think I look like her, too?"

The face under the horrible hat was a young, pretty one. Dezzy looked up into Grandpa's old, wrinkled face and said she couldn't see any resemblance.

"I mean when I was younger, Dezzy. After all, Mickey looks like me, and Dee looks like Mickey. Yes, I think she's my grandmother. That's who she is."

"But, Grandpa, didn't you know your grandmother?"

"No." Grandpa was smiling at the picture now. "She died young, poor thing—some kind of sickness they couldn't handle then. But everybody said she was nice as could be, and I was the spitting image of her. Yes, that's who she is—my grandmother."

"I don't think she was so nice if she wore a dead bird on her head," Dezzy said in a mean voice.

Grandpa didn't hear her. "I haven't seen this picture in years," he said happily. "And it makes you feel good to think that some things don't change. It's the same face Dee has. Maybe I should frame it and hang it up."

"I wouldn't hang up a picture of somebody who liked dead birds," Dezzy said in a louder voice.

Grandpa turned to look at her. "What is it with you, Dezzy? Can't I enjoy looking at a picture of my own grandmother?"

"It's only because she looks like Dee," Dezzy snapped. "You think it's so great that Dee looks like your side of the family. Well, I don't look like your side of the family, and I'm glad."

"Hey!" Grandpa grinned. "You're jealous of Dee, and you're jealous of my grandmother's picture."

"I am not," Dezzy snarled. "I wouldn't want to look like a weirdo woman who likes dead birds."

"You are some nut case, Dezzy." Grandpa shook his head, and she scowled up at him. "But I guess

you can't help yourself. You may not look like me or
my grandmother, but you sure do act like me—stub-
born, pigheaded, and stupid." He put an arm around
her, and she stopped scowling and leaned her head
on his shoulder.

"Do you really think I'm like you, Grandpa?" she
asked finally.

"No question."

"And I'm never going to change."

They both watched the game for a while, and then
Dezzy said, "Go ahead and frame the picture,
Grandpa. I won't mind."

"Shut up," he said. "Can't you see the bases are
loaded?"

Mom and Dad returned, bubbling over with stories about their cruise and with lots of boring information about Alaska. They brought back snapshots and curios—wood carvings done by some of the Indians who lived up there and little totem poles, one for Dee and one for Dezzy.

"The Pacific Northwest Indians were the most gifted wood-carvers of all the Native American tribes," Dad said. Dad always learned a great deal on any trip he took and kept talking about it until he went away on a new trip.

He showed Dezzy a pamphlet on totem poles. It

had pictures of real totem poles and old, old photos of some of the Indians who had carved them. Dad told her that the coming of the white man brought about the death of many of those Indians.

"Why?" Dezzy wanted to know. She had been thinking about death a lot ever since Grandma died.

"I'm sure you must have studied this in school, Dezzy," Dad said. "You know that Indians all across this country were conquered and killed in one way or another by the white man."

"But why?" Dezzy wanted to know.

"I don't know why exactly, Dezzy, but that's the way it's always been. Somebody is always wanting what somebody else has, and lots of people down the ages have died because of war and disease."

"I hope I die of old age," Dezzy said. "I don't want to die because of war and disease."

"We all hope so." Dad laughed. "But I don't think you need to worry about it."

"Why not?" Dezzy insisted. "Everybody should worry about it."

Dad didn't worry. Neither did Mom. It should have comforted Dezzy that neither of her parents worried about death. They were a lot closer to it than she was, if you went by age. Still, she found herself thinking about death and dying. One day, she would die. She hated thinking that the world would just go on without her. She wondered if Grandma had felt the same way, and if Grandpa's grandmother had also felt that way. And those Indians, those wonderful woodcarvers, who hadn't planned on dying. How had they felt?

A letter came from Joey. He had received his package and loved everything in it. He said he wore his Groucho Marx mask everywhere, much to the disgust of his older brother. He had scooted the toy mouse across the floor and his mother had run shrieking from the room. He had also offered the can of peanuts to his mother's boyfriend, whose name was Terry. When the snake jumped out, Terry had practically fallen off his chair. Then he said that Joey should never do that to grown-ups because it could cause a heart attack. All in all, Joey said, he loved his birthday present. He wanted to know what they thought of the package he had sent them.

"Maybe it got lost in the mail," Dezzy suggested.

"He'll probably be back long before it comes,"

Grandpa said. "The post office gets worse and worse every year."

"Was it better when you were a boy, Grandpa?"

"It sure was," Grandpa said. "We used to get two deliveries a day. One in the morning and one in the afternoon. It was a lot better."

"But Dad said they killed a lot of Indians back then."

"That was before my time," Grandpa said.

Dezzy thought about Grandpa's wedding picture and about the uniform he was wearing. "Did you ever kill anybody, Grandpa?" she wanted to know.

"Nope," Grandpa said. "But I have to admit there were times I would have liked to."

"When you were a soldier, Grandpa. Then did you kill anybody?"

"No, I didn't," Grandpa said. "I never even got out of this country. Most of the time I spent fixing jeeps and wanting to kill the sergeant in my division." Grandpa laughed. "That guy was a real little Caesar."

"Grandpa, do you think you ever could have killed anybody? If you had been sent away to fight, could you have killed anybody?"

"Go away," Grandpa said. "Can't you see I'm busy?"

- - -

Dezzy's ankle hurt. Sometimes it woke her up at night, and she couldn't get comfortable whichever way she turned.

"A few more weeks now," Mom said, "and they'll take the cast off. You've been great, Dezzy. Just hang in a little bit longer."

Sometimes when Dezzy lay there at night, unable to sleep, she thought about death. Sometimes she grew so frightened, she thought about waking up Mom and Dad and jumping into bed with them the way she had when she was little.

She put on the light sometimes and looked around her room at all the pictures of her and Dee, hanging up on the walls. She wondered if one day somebody not even born yet would come and sleep in her room and look at the pictures the way she had this summer in Dad's old room. Everything had changed so much for her this summer—Grandma dead, Dee away by herself in camp, her foot aching in a cast, thinking different kinds of thoughts from what she'd thought before. She thought about the past, and she worried about the future. Was there going to be a future for her? When would she die?

Sometimes it was very scary, and she wanted to wake up Mom or Dad. But she never did.

Joey's package finally arrived. It was a small one and contained only a gold-colored watch chain for Grandpa and a big white button, slightly scraped, with green trees on it and words that said SAVE OUR TREES.

"I used to have a pocket watch," Grandpa said. "I don't know what happened to it."

"You should look for it, Grandpa, now that you have a gold watch chain."

"I don't think it's real gold," Grandpa said. "And besides, I never really liked the pocket watch. But it was very thoughtful of Joey to think of us."

Dezzy held her button up. "I wonder why he sent me this," she said.

"Well, I guess he found it, and it's a nice-looking button, and he figures that you're into saving birds, so why not forests?"

"I never thought about forests," Dezzy said, but she pinned on the button and liked hearing it rattle when she moved around.

• • •

Dee's letters grew happier and happier. She loved camp. She loved the plays they put on. She had a big part as somebody's bossy mother in the final production. The somebody was a boy named Ryan. He lived in Berkeley and was fourteen and a half. She was sorry Dezzy was having such a miserable summer. Maybe next year they could both go to Camp Cornell.

"I'm not having a miserable summer," Dezzy told Grandpa as they cruised around the park one morning. "I'm just doing a lot of thinking."

"Don't do too much," Grandpa said. "You ought to watch more TV."

"Too much TV gives me a headache. And besides, I don't mind thinking, although sometimes it scares me. I'm trying to decide what I should do with my life. I'd really like to do something important, so that when I die what I did will make a difference. Maybe I could do something that will help birds or maybe forests or maybe even people. It's very hard to decide."

"You've got plenty of time," Grandpa said. "Maybe right now you should try to have more fun. Why don't you get together with some of your girlfriends?"

"I only have one girlfriend—Rachel Castori. She's

away at camp, but, you know, Grandpa, she never even sent me a card. I wrote to her twice, but she never answered."

"Some friend!" Grandpa said, and began blowing his horn because the car in front of him and the car in front of that were blowing their horns.

"I'm going to stop calling her mother," Dezzy said. "Maybe I'll even stop being friends with her."

"I never had many friends either," Grandpa said. "I wonder when Joey's coming back."

C H A P T E R

Dezzy didn't cry when they removed the cast, even though her ankle still hurt. She didn't cry when she couldn't jog at first because her ankle was too stiff and tender. And she didn't cry when Dee made fun of her.

"You really are a weirdo," Dee said. She had returned from camp with long hair, lots of eye makeup, and a funny way of talking.

"Go away!" Dezzy said. "Can't you see I'm busy?"

"You sound like Grandpa." Dee's voice rose. "You've been hanging around him too long, and you're getting to be just like him."

Dezzy was working on a design for a trash can. Her group, Youth for Environmental Safety (YES), was sponsoring a trash-can contest. Joey had submitted a very funny one, showing the backs of different kinds of people—fat people, skinny people, tall ones, short ones—all trying to look inside the can. Dezzy's design was a very simple one, since she was not a good artist. The lower part of the can was painted black like a shark's body, with jagged pointed teeth all around the opening as if it were a mouth.

"I am a lot like Grandpa," Dezzy agreed.

Dee tossed her long blond hair. Her dangling earrings tinkled. Nowadays she hung out with a crowd of kids who wore only stylish black-and-white clothes. "What's that supposed to be anyway?"

"It's supposed to be a shark's mouth."

"It doesn't look like a shark's mouth."

Dezzy didn't answer. She started coloring in the teeth with a white marking pen.

"What a stupid idea for a contest," Dee said. "All my friends think you're crazy."

"Shut up, Dee!" Dezzy said. "I'm busy."

●   ●   ●

The YES kids cleaned up the school yard and set out recycling bins for aluminum cans, papers, and plastics. They planned to fan out into the neighborhood, the park, and maybe the beaches, too. Ms. Finkelstein said that the school could not be responsible for them after school hours. She wondered if the PTA might want to sponsor some of their activities.

Grandpa agreed to be one of the sponsors. As long as he could cruise along after them in his car and didn't have to collect garbage himself, he was willing to help out.

Ms. Finkelstein was surprised at the interest in YES. Twenty-three kids formed its core. Some came because they cared about animals; others worried about the greenhouse effect, pollution, the ozone layer. . . . Lenny Gee said he wanted to be sure the earth didn't die before he did. Amanda Fonzi said she was afraid the world would become one great big garbage dump if people didn't learn to recycle. Dezzy wasn't the only one who worried about the effect of garbage on birds. Some kids, like Joey, weren't clear on exactly what their reasons were for joining. Jack Gonzalez, for instance, wasn't as enthusiastic about saving the environment as he was about

having an opportunity to draw and paint. He was
the one who came up with the idea of running a trash-
can contest. He was also the one who did most of the
YES posters that hung all over the school. The poster
Dezzy liked best showed a mountain of garbage—
shoes, cans, paper cups, banners, spaghetti, boxes,
chicken bones. At the top, only a piece of a redhead
and a few arms waving desperately were all that
remained of people. DON'T LET THIS HAPPEN TO YOU
was printed in bright rainbow colors. JOIN YES.

Mr. Franklin bumped into Dezzy one day as she was
hurrying through the hall. Her ankle was feeling
much more flexible, and she was wondering if she
might try jogging in the park that afternoon. She
was pretty sure Grandpa would be available, and
she was almost certain that Joey would be, too. She
put up her hand to touch the gold chain, which she
wore most of the time these days. She was glad to
have a friend like Joey.

"Oh, hello there, Dezzy," Mr. Franklin said as they
both arranged themselves after bumping. He wasn't
her science teacher any longer. Now she had Ms.
Crawford, who was much more boring.

"Hello, Mr. Franklin." Dezzy smiled at him. She liked Mr. Franklin and appreciated the C minus.

"I'm glad to see you, Dezzy, because I really am impressed with your YES group. It's wonderful to know that there are some kids your age who are concerned with the environment and are doing something about it."

"They're a great bunch of kids," Dezzy agreed.

Mr. Franklin hesitated. "You know, Dezzy, sometimes I think I may have made a mistake with the mark I gave you last term."

Dezzy sighed. "I was afraid you might feel that way."

Mr. Franklin said earnestly, "I always felt that my best students were the ones who did well on tests and reports. But maybe there are others, like you, who apply the principles of science in a practical way."

The bell rang, and Dezzy flexed herself for a sprint to her next class. Sometimes the teachers didn't mark you late if you got inside the door within a couple of minutes after the bell rang.

But Mr. Franklin continued talking. "Maybe we have to appreciate the doers as well as the thinkers."

"I think I'm going to be late, Mr. Franklin," Dezzy said desperately.

"Maybe"—Mr. Franklin didn't seem to hear her— "maybe it's wrong to even try to separate people into thinkers and doers. Maybe it's the finished work that should be appreciated. Anyway, Dezzy, I do think I could have given you a higher mark. Certainly a C or even a B minus. You've made a difference."

Dezzy ended up being late. As punishment she had to help clean up the school yard during lunchtime. But since she would have been doing that anyway, she didn't mind.

16

Dezzy didn't want a birthday party.

"What I'd really like," she said, "is to have a big picnic out at Stinson Beach. There's a bird sanctuary not far from there, and we could see blue herons and snowy egrets. Then we could eat lunch and, later, hang out on the beach. Most of the kids in my YES group would like to come, and I think we could get some parents to drive us."

"Absolutely not!" said Dee. "What I'd like is a real party—boys and girls this time." Dee grinned. "We could have it downstairs in the basement, string up some decorations and lights. I'll invite some kids from school and maybe a few others."

Dezzy knew that Dee was thinking of Ryan Marcus, who lived in Berkeley, and a couple of other kids she'd met at Camp Cornell.

"We could have Cokes or other soft drinks—"

"Yuck!"

"—and platters of stuff from the deli—"

"Yuck!"

"We could play music and dance. Come on, Dezzy, you could invite Joe and some of the other kids in your weirdo YES group."

"Most of them don't drink Cokes anymore—and some of them are vegetarians."

"Well, I'm not going on any nutty bird-watching picnic."

"And I'm not going to any tacky party."

Of course, they compromised. Dee and most of her friends, including Ryan Marcus, came on the picnic to Stinson Beach. It turned out that Ryan was interested in birds as well as acting. Most of the kids loved playing on the clean sandy beach and splashing in the water. Dezzy jogged by herself along the beach and didn't notice her ankle at all. She stopped about half a mile away from the others and looked back at all her friends and family enjoying themselves on her birthday. She didn't think at all about death or dying.

That same night, a bunch of sunburned kids, some wearing stylish black-and-white pants and tops, others wearing clothes that weren't stylish, held a party in Dee and Dezzy's basement. Earlier, some of them had helped decorate and hang lights. Others had collected CDs or arranged the food and drinks. When the party began, the stylish group and the unstylish one started out separate but mingled as the evening progressed. Some of the kids danced, laughed, and sang along with the music. Others ate, talked, or sat quietly, looking on.

Dezzy did all of the above, ending up, finally, sitting quietly next to Joey.

"Your sister's okay," Joey said. "She's nothing like you, and she talks phony. But she's okay."

Joey's ears were bright red. Otherwise, he wasn't sunburned at all. His ears were the one place he had forgotten to cover with sun block.

Dezzy giggled.

"What's so funny?" Joey wanted to know.

"Your ears," she said. "You're the first person I ever met who got sunburned on his ears."

"Shut up!" Joey said, taking her hand. "Can't you see I'm busy?"